Must I Tell It?

I Gotta Tell It!

ADDIE JUNE HALL, Ph.D.

Must I Tell It?
I Gotta Tell It!

Must I Tell It?
I Gotta Tell It!

A Book of Sermons
That Are Promoting, Pronouncing,
Propelling, Prospering and Providential

Addie June Hall, Ph. D.

ARPress
45 Dan Road Suite 5
Canton MA 02021

Hotline: 1(888) 821-0229
Fax: 1(508) 545-7580

Ordering Information:
Quantity sales. Special discounts are available on quantity purchases by corporations, associations, and others. For details, contact the publisher at the address above.

Printed in the United States of America.

ISBN-13:   Paperback   979-8-89389-618-3
             eBook   979-8-89389-619-0

Library of Congress Control Number: 2024921321

CONTENTS

FOREWORD

The preacher is the vehicle of practical theology. One aspect of this medium is the area or preaching. Preaching has been and will continue to be the hallmark of hope and the pivot of promises. It brings life to all who are open to receive the Word of God and to hear from the holy heaven.

Contrary to this fact, it appears that we are retracting from the traditional preaching. We are afraid to preach the consequences of sin from the pulpits. 'We are afraid to rock the boat. We are afraid that our members will not like our preaching about sin and that we will lose them; we are also afraid that our money will dry up, or feelings will be hurt. Are we to sacrifice the Word of God for temporal gifts? l hope not! When have you heard a sermon on adultery, fornication, or any of the Ten Commandments in your church? If recently, then praise God. I have heard ministers say that adultery and fornication are not a part of the ministries. An exact, quote from a well-respected Evangelist follows: "I read your book, but all of us have different ministries, and teaching about adultery or fornication is not a part of our ministry." Another teacher of the Word replicated that statement using different terminology. Did Jesus teach on these subjects? Are we to follow Jesus' footsteps? Where are the true worshippers of God? Each one of those preachers asked that I send a donation to his or her ministry. The prophets and preachers of age preached about sin and gave words of assurance, deliverance and hope for seemingly hopeless situations. There are some modern day prophets, pastors and evangelists who are not afraid to call sin – sin. One such man (among other men and women) is Dr. Bill Bougknight who penned the following words within his sermon How Do ight who penned the following words within his sermon How Do You

Measure Greatness? In doing so he called the Sermon Topic "It's Not All That Bad." The illustration from that sermon is provided for your reading.

Most nice respectable American churches don't talk about sin, judgment, or hell. Why? Because they are post-modern. Most Americans read the Bible selectively, omitting those parts they don't like. The first thing many American churchgoers throw out is the concept of hell, because (in their view) a nice, well-behaved God wouldn't let anybody go to hell. After you lose hell, you lose a sense of sin. Nobody is guilty of anything. Everybody is just a victim. Finally, the call to repent has no meaning. Dr. Calvin Miller of the Beeson Divinity School claims that instead of repenting we play a nice little game entitled "It's not all that bad." It sounds like this:

"Yes, I did have a brief affair, but my wife was not meeting my needs. I didn't divorce her, so don't call it adultery; It's not all that bad."

"Yes, my daughter and her fiancé share the same bedroom when they visit us, but most engaged couples do. After all, this is the 21st century; it's not all that bad."

"Sure, I sometimes drink too much, but never in front of the kids. I don't want any harm and it never causes me to miss a day of work. It's not all that bad."

Some time ago, Dr. Bougknight stated that he once read a cartoon which stated that when Charlie Brown did something wrong, he feels entitlement. What a huge moral slippage this example reveals in our culture. Jesus' messages of good news always began with "repent." "Repent, for the kingdom of God is at hand" (Matthew 4:17). Jesus bragged on a notorious sinner who was a tax collector. A prayer of repentance always rings bells in heaven (Luke 18:10-14). The greatness of this tax collector was that he knew how to repent, how to say, I'm sorry." All of us can be forgiven if we are humble enough to say, "I'm sorry."

[The above illustrations were given by Dr. Bougknight and appeared in June 24, 2001 Sermon illustrations on www.sermons.com]

Dr. Olin P. Moyd, author of The Sacred Arts, contends that the need for profound belief in God and personal salvation are the important issues of Christianity; however, the methodology for achieving those objectives should be modeled on the method of Jesus (himself). Jesus encountered persons at the point of their needs (p.5).

Dr. J. Deoris Roberts, Sr. a senior theologian and author, recounts his experience in Black Theology in Dialogue: "We must in no way abandon an intense concern for personal sin and salvation. We are becoming aware, however, that sinful social structures often destroy persons, families and communities" (p.84).

Nations are destroyed because of sin. It is a sin not to preach about sin. We are to continue to preach liberation and not enslavement, and we must ask God for holy boldness in our preaching. Having taken a class in Black Preaching where there were only five black persons in the class and twenty persons of other ethnicities, I observed the methodology employed by all. I am aware that I black preacher has always had a viable and potent influence on black parishioners and non-black parishioners as well.

Dr. Walter B. Hoard, author of Outstanding Black Sermons, Vol. 2, writes, "A preacher can be forgiven of any sin by his congregation except failing to preach well." Hoard continues, "As the black preacher goes, so goes the race. He or she is the earthly epitome of God. Essentials are, did the sermon help someone know God better? Did the sermon improve someone's lifestyle?" (pp.12,13).

Dr. Henry H. Mitchell in speaking of the black preacher said, "The black preacher is not an army officer ordering men to their death. Rather he [or she) is a crucial witness declaring how men (humans) ought to live" (p.203). Black Preaching, New York, N.Y p. 203.

God looks upon the heart. Sometimes, God in His mighty wisdom and in His goodness seeks the least of us so that His grace may appear the more glorious. You see, God uses ordinary persons, willing persons to accomplish His work. Thus, I was led co share a group of sermons with you, to have God speak to you, edify you, and empower you at this moment. I am one of the least ones who heard His call. He has laid His hands on me and I must do His will. I have a passion for telling it like it is. Yes, my passion is Jesus Christ, the Anointed One, and telling all who will hear, listen or read about Jesus. This is the apex of this book.

It is my desire and my Father's desire that each of us should experience a deeper relationship, a deeper level, and a deeper commitment with Jesus the Christ.

To my children, Ms. Sharmane Hall, Dr. and Mrs. LeRoy B. Hall, Jr. (Earnestine); my brother, Mr. and Mrs. Allen Ware (Carolyn) and family; my nieces and nephews; and all of my family, and my friends, thanks for your support. "We will forever serve the Lord with true humility and respect."

To all of you, Jesus died chat we may have life more abundantly. Ask for it, believe and receive it.

To all whom I have quoted, thank you for your inspiration, your eloquence, your gifts and talents.

To the Reverend Kathy Clark, thank you for reading the first draft and for your suggestions. Your reward from God is great.

I give special thanks to my indefatigable friend and sister Link, Professor Mamie Hixon, for proofreading and correcting of this manuscript.

I am greatly indebted to Mrs. Evelyn Kelker for proofreading this manuscript and to Mrs. Mary Scott for her willingness to type if needed.

To my friends and technology specialists, Michael Hual and Clint Morgan, thanks for all of your encouragement and technological help in working with this project. I am greatly indebted to you as well.

To Julius Jordan, the technology specialist who is always here for me, my appreciation is extended for your assistance in getting this on the Internet.

To Dr. Karl Stegall, former Pastor of First United Methodist Church in Montgomery, you are definitely special in the eyes of God; you are following the Master's command. Thank you for encouraging me and sharing your kindness and your affirmations with me, the least of His. Thanks for having your church support me during my seminary studies.

To the Goodwyn family and the Thompson family, thank you for your acts of kindness during my seminary experience. May God continue to shower blessings upon you and yours. Thank you so very much. Money spent for God's work is banked in your heavenly account.

To all of you, may the power of Almighty God be realized in its full glory, unimpeded by doubt and unweakened by skepticism couching all who are in need.

To those who constantly prayed for me and encouraged me, when I could have so easily given up, God shall continue to reward you. Believe it!

TO GOD BE THE GLORY
"HALLOWED BE THY NAME"

INTRODUCTION

MUST I TELL IT? I GOTTA TELL IT!

Must I Tell It? Our son between the ages of three through five frequently voiced these words: "Must I Tell let' Essentially, he would always wait until after the grace had been offered at the dinner cable to reveal chose things he wanted to tell. His father and I would search our minds to recall what we had done to contribute to the upcoming revelation. When one of us would recall an incident, chat one would say, "No, boy, eat your dinner." However, the child was not satisfied until the other spouse said, "It's all right to tell it." Then he would commence to cell his story. Once he said, "Guess where daddy and I went."

I would reply, "Where?'"

He continued, "to the score." He spoke to a lady and they talked a long time, and he drove her home."

Another time after, "a must I tell it," he said, "Guess what mom and I did." That was my cue to tell him to eat his dinner.

His father said, "What?"

He replied, "We went to the post office and she sent a money order back to the United States." His father asked to whom? He wasn't able to fill in the details, but he had to tell where we went.

Another time, his father took him to a different store and when our neighbor asked him where he had been, his reply was that he had been to a store with his father. The neighbor said, "I don't see any packages."

The child said, "The package is in his pocket under his jacket."

His father replied, "I am not taking you any where if you got to tell it." The child had to tell it! And having told it, he was satisfied.

My friends in Christ, I MUST TELL IT! I have a command from the Master to tell it. I am going to tell it! I GOTTA TELL IT! Jesus told His disciples, "All authority has been given to me in heaven and on earth." "Go therefore and make disciples of all nations, baptizing chem in the name of the Father and of the Son and of the Holy Spirit, teaching them to observe all things chat I have commanded you; and lo I am with you always, even to the end of age" (Matthew 28:18-20). "GO" implies chat believers are to be active and aggressive in winning the lost, shaking and awaking the comfortable, and bringing hope co those who are in need of hope.

Personally, God has given me this command to share His Word, and I shall obey Him. I pray chat chis writing, this work will speak to you and bless your soul, in Jesus' name. MUST I TELL IT! I GOTTA TO TELL IT!

LOVE YOUR WIFE and
SAVE YOUR LIFE

SCRIPTURE: MATTHEW 19:4-6

And He answered and said to them, "Have you not read that He who made them at the beginning 'made them male and female,'

"And said, 'For this reason a man shall leave his father and mother and be joined to his wife, and the two shall become one flesh?

"So then, they are no longer two but one flesh. Therefore what God has joined together, let not man separate."

SHE BELIEVED YOU WHEN YOU SAID IN A LOW
BARITONE VOICE, "BABY, I'LL ALWAYS LOVE YOU"
WHEN YOU PLAYED, TIME OUT FOR TEARS,
MY DARLING, I'M WAITING FOR YOU;

WHEN YOU PROMISED, "I'LL BE WITH YOU FOREVER."
SHE BELIEVED YOU ---AND YOU WALKED AWAY.

YOU BELIEVED HER WHEN SHE SAID,
"I DON'T BELIEVE IN DIVORCE." WHEN SHE SAID,
"YOU ARE MY DREAM MAN."

YOU BELIEVED HER ------ BUT SHE LEFT ANYWAY.

You didn't believe God when He said to love your wife as Christ loves the Church. Neither did you hear the Master ask, "Have you not read that He who made them at the beginning made them 'male and female,'... for this reason a man shall leave his father and mother and be joined to his wife, and the two shall become ONE FLESH"?

WHAT DO YOU BELIEVE? LET ME GIVE YOU SOME TRUTHS...

John was placed in prison and killed for his public opinions on marriage and divorce, and the Pharisees hoped to trap Jesus, too. They were trying to trick Jesus by having him choose sides in a theological controversy. There were two main groups that had opposing views of divorce. One group supported divorce for almost any reason. Does this scenario sound familiar? The other group believed divorce could be allowed only for marital unfaithfulness. But Jesus in his answer focused on marriage rather than divorce. He pointed out that Scripture intended marriage to be permanent, Matthew 19, verses 1-6.

Brothers and sisters, life hasn't been easy for the man or woman, who has been rejected and left with children to raise. Many of us can identify with this situation. All across North America (and it is not restricted to North America), people are seeking counselors, calling for prayers, calling pastors and anyone else, lamenting because a spouse has satisfied his or her selfish desire to abandon his or her family. This abandonment has caused hurt to whoever is left behind. It has changed the direction of many lives. Recently, on a popular talk show, men and women lamented over the anger and pain they imposed upon their families. Realizing their sins, many stated that if they were able to relive their lives that they would not make that same mistake. Some cried and asked their children and former spouses to forgive them. Asking for forgiveness is a good thing. Why? The Bible tells us that the wages of sin is death. Sin pays wages, and those wages are eternal. Next, forgiveness is limited not by the amount of sin, but our willingness to repent. And most important, God made Jesus who knew no sin to be sin for us, that we might become the righteousness of God in Him (2 Corinthian 5:21). Ephesians 1:7 tells us "In Him we have redemption through His blood, the forgiveness of sins, according to the riches of His grace." My friends, we must repent and ask for God's forgiveness.

Conversely, there are those who remain in marriages that are filled with envy, jealousy, unforgiveness, infidelity, adultery and abuse, both psychological and physical. TIlese are marriages that are painful. I have talked with and received communications from women and men of various ethnicities, religious persuasions, ages, and incomes and all bring to the table similar stories. Nevertheless, my task for this moment is to focus on women who are composites of many women who have suffered or are suffering from the devil's intervention in their marriages. Men, I know some of you are hurting or have been hurt as well. This sermon will speak to you also. Remember when Peter was preaching to Cornelius' household, Peter said, "I see very clearly that the Jews are not God's only favorites" (Acts 10:34). TIlis Scripture is applicable to male and female. God does not show partiality. Whoever fears Him and works righteously is accepted by Him (Acts 10:35).

Now to those of you who are committing adultery, I have told you that God said, "TIle wages of sin is death." Stop it and Live!

Women love your own husband! Men love your own wife! We have only to pick up our daily newspapers or look at television to see the suffering this infidelity is imposing on families and society as a whole. All of us pay for this evil.

Throughout history, there were women forced into adultery, not voluntarily but forcibly, and they were denied their human rights. God forbid that this is happening, today. I am an advocate for healthy marriages. I will speak against adultery, its destructive forces and the healing process that channel men, women and children through any traumatic, excruciating experience. I shall begin with the healing book, the Bible.

Reading the story of Hagar within the Bible, one would view Hagar, the other woman, not as a volunteer but as the other woman by command. We are told that Hagar was uprooted from Egypt. She was taken from her African heritage. Does this remind you of the African-American woman? It should because history compares the African-American woman to Hagar. Genesis 16:6 reminds us that Hagar was introduced as the solution to a problem confronting a wealthy Hebrew slave-holding family composed of Sarai (Hagar's owner) and Abram, Sarai's husband. The Bible tells us that Sarai was barren and had borne no children. But she had a slave-girl called

Hager. So Sarai said to Abram, "Listen, Now! 'Since Yahweh has not given me any children,' go to my slave-girl. Perhaps I shall get children through her." And Abram took Sarai's advice. But the other woman was not the wife and trouble would soon surface. After Abram and Hagar obeyed Sarai, the struggle between the powerful and powerless began. This power struggle in human relationships disrupted peace in the family unit, a whole nation, and this disruption is continuing in this millennium.

After surveying hundreds of men regarding men seeking intimate relationships with other women, I received many responses. In this sermon, I will name only a few of the reason given: To fill the void that is sometimes existing in a relationship, ego-building, emotional support, not receiving love and affection at home, always being criticized by the wife, no support from wife, and many other excuses as listed in my book The Wife I The Other Woman. These excuses will not be accepted by God. Cheating is wrong! It is not accepted by God. God said, "Thou shall not commit Adultery."

The Bible is God's sex manual for married couples. Proverbs 5:15-23 highlights God's pleasure principle. Proverbs 5:15: Marriage is God's divine antidote for sexual temptation. Proverbs 5:16-17: God designed and preserved sexuality for marriage. Proverbs 20-23: God has also designed a system of checks and balances for chose succumbing to sexual temptation. He sees all and will punish chose who violate His sovereign plan.

God's ideal plan for marriage is one man for one woman for one lifetime. God's pattern for marital happiness is evident when a man loves and leads his family, with children who obey and revere their parents (Ephesians 6:1-4), with a wife who respects and supports her husband's leadership (Ephesians 5:21-23). A mutually supportive attitude must characterize both husband and wife if they are to succeed in building a harmonious home. In marriage, you are one. Love one another.

Permit me co ask both men and women the questions chat follow: Are you sending your spouse into the arms of another person? Are you giving him or her an excuse to sin? Hagar didn't have a choice to refuse her owner's request. The women in slavery didn't have a choice to refuse the slave masters. Are you in slavery? No, you have a choice. Are you letting saran (I refuse to capitalize his name) make a choice for you? Are you making your master the devil? God said, "Adultery, fornication and lust are sins." Do you chink no one knows of your sin? Some one knows. Even if your adulterous sin is a secret, secret sins are open scandals to God. Do you know chat your body is rhe temple of the Holy Spirit who is in you, whom you have from God, and you are not of your own (1 Cor. 6:19)? My book tided The Wife I The Other Woman also addressed adultery and its destructive forces as well as other pertinent issues relevant to marriage. I discovered that eighty-five percent of all America's problems are the result of dysfunctional families in which men and some women have neglected or left their spouses and children. Most of these break-ups stem from infidelity. A life of adultery will make one forsake his or her children and his or her spouse. Then comes the divorce!

Most writers will concur with me when I say that the trauma of divorce is comparable to the trauma of death. It is a death of a marriage usually caused by selfishness. Dr. Hart wrote in his book Growing up Divorced that for a while he wondered if he had overstated the case of the scars of divorce. He continued by saying that he was speaking personally, as someone who had experienced the pain as a child. In my book, Ike Wife / "ihe Other Woman, the reader will experience the pain that prevails for years within the lives of many. Concurrently, during the many years that I taught psychology, I listened to students talk about the trauma they experienced when their fathers left their mothers. If only they realize that this selfishness hurts all involved. Yes all, even the other woman or the other man. Looking back on my own experience, I saw how God took a bad situation and turned it into a blessing. I am truly blessed. Let me say that all children need a father figure in their lives. This point I still maintain. When fathers fail, nations fail! Yet, let us not forget to thank God for praying mothers, who through it all are able to raise respectable, hard-working children, when left alone to do so.

In the New Testament, Jesus and the Apostles talked about divorce. Jesus told the Pharisees that because of the hardness of . their hearts, Moses allowed bills of divorcement, but reminded them this was not the intent of God. The Apostle Paul, at the request of the believers in the Church at Corinth where sexual immorality abounded, said, "It is good for a man not to touch a woman! Nevertheless, because of sexual immorality, let each man have his own wife, and let each woman have her own husband (1Cor. 7:1-3). Furthermore, this chapter tells you how to live as you are called and gives advice to the unmarried and widows.

Church, the judgment that begins in the house has reached our cities and is prevalent in all parts of our society. Infidelity is a dreadful sin in the eyes of Almighty God. It leads to the deterioration of a nation. Men, you don't have to commit adultery! Love your wife and save your life! Women, you don't have to commit adultery! Love your own husband and save your life! It is not wise to let your eyes do your thinking for you.

Work with - not against God
Work with - not against your spouse
Work with - not against your children
Work with - not against your community, your state, your Nation

Satisfy not your selfish desire and destroy the lives of others.

Many years ago, The famed Motown Singers, 1he Temptations sang, "I want a love I can see. I don't want a love you have to tell me about. That's the Kind of love I can do without." The Apostle Paul reminds us to exhibit a love that others can see and feel. That's the kind of love husbands and wives should give each other. However, chis type of love is impossible without your loving God first. "For this is the message chat you heard from the beginning that we should love one another" (1 John 3:11).

GOD SAID, "THOU SHALL NOT KILL."

Thou shall not kill! Have you killed the hopes, the inspirations of chose who trusted you? If so you muse repent. Repent before it is too late. God will hear you and forgive you. II Chronicles 7:14 says, "If my people who are called by my name will humble themselves, and pray and seek my face, and turn from their wicked ways, then I will hear from heaven, and will forgive their sins and heal their land."

I know we need a healing of the land. Look all around you. Can't you see that we need a healing of the land? This is a clarion call for all of God's people to call upon God and ask God to heal the land. If you belong to God, you have the power to speak and it shall be done.

FORGIVE AND BE FORGIVEN

Are you a forgiving person? God is a forgiving God. I have heard people ask why should I forgive…? He or she hurt me, badly. Forgive because God says to forgive. In the Lord's Prayer, we ask God to "forgive us our debts, as we forgive our debtors" (Matt. 6:12). This prayer comes with a promise. If we forgive others for their transgressions, our Creator will forgive us. But if we do not forgive, neither are we forgiven.

Forgiveness tears down all walls between you and the person who offended you. Forgiveness frees you and it frees the offender. It opens the door for God to alleviate the pain or hurt experienced. God and only God can and will heal you or the person you hurt. In Hebrew language "forgive" means "to cut loose." Cut loose, release those who hurt you. Forgive them and forgive yourself. We are told to forgive others as Christ has forgiven us, for the love of God is shed abroad in our hearts by the Holy Ghost. We must free ourselves from unforgiveness and strife. What is forgiveness?

Dr. Adams in his writing From Forgiven to Forgiving said that forgiveness is a promise. When God forgives us, He promised that He will not remember our sins against us anymore! Dr. Adams further stated that forgetting 15 passive and is something that we human beings, not being omniscient, do. 'Not remember' is active; it is a promise whereby one person determines not to remember the sins of another against him. To 'Not remember' is simply a graphic way of saying, will not bring up these matters to you or others in the future. I will bury them and not exhume the bones to beat you over the head with them.' I will never use these sins against you." p.3

Have you truly forgiven those who are in need of your forgiveness? Thank God for His resurrection! Because He lives and forgives the repentant heart, we can live and forgive, too.

"And when you were dead in your trespasses and uncircumcised of the flesh, He has made you alive together with Him, having forgiven you all trespasses, having wiped out the handwriting of requirements that was against us, and He has taken it out of the way, having nailed it to the cross" (Colossians 2:13-14).

Again, God speaks to the circumstances. "I, even I am He that blotteth out thy transgressions for mine sake, and will not remember thy sins" Jeremiah 31:34b). God is a forgiving God. He just told you so.

Mark 11:25 says, "When you pray, if you have anything against anyone, forgive them so that God may forgive you." TI1ere are children out there that lose a parent or were rejected by a parent. Forgive that parent. Some may have been abused; don't hold on to that abuse. Let it go! God can and will take away the bitterness, the hurt, the anger and even the hatred. Ask God to do that for you. Make a decision to forgive. Let God's love make the difference in your life.

Husbands, pray for your wives; and, wives pray for your husbands. Husbands and wives chat pray together will overcome any difficulty that they may face.

God said, "Love one another." He who loves is of God.
God said, "Bless one another." The blessings you send out will return
    to you.
God said, "Respect one another." How can you not respect your body?
    The two of you became one.
God said, "Touch one another." Sleep together. Physical closeness is
    essential. You are married.
God said, "Hear My Word and Obey Me." If you love God, you will
    obey God.

I know that life can't always be "picture perfect." Seek Gods' guidance. Hebrews 13:4 tells us, "Marriage is honorable in all." Remember this Scripture and try harder to grow together in love, understanding and faith. Again, I say communicate with your feelings. Stop holding feelings within you that need to be communicated. Follow the examples of Christ who was unselfish, giving his best to us that we may give our best to others. Find joy in your marriage and thank God for each other.

Success in marriage is more than finding the right person. It is being the right person. A successful marriage is built on the Word of God and your relationship with God. A successful marriage is one where the husband and wife submit to one another in fear of God. A successful marriage is built on good communication which includes talking (sharing your feelings), listening (attentively listening), and understanding what the communication is saying. Proverbs 3:13 says, "Blessed is the man who finds wisdom, the man who gains understanding."

Husbands, love you wives, just as Christ also loved the Church and gave Himself for her, that He might sanctify and cleanse her with the washing of water by the word (Ephesians 5:25, 26).

Wives, submit to your own husbands, as to the Lord (Ephesians 5:22).

Froehle said, and I concur, "As Incredible as it seems, God depends on each of us to speak what needs to be said. God puts words of comfort, encouragement and love in our mouths: Use them to bless others.

I read that a man visited God's storehouse which was filled with many marvelous gifts for mankind. I will paraphrase this story. The man approached the angels in charge of the storehouse and said, "Madam and Sir, I am so tired of miseries of life on earth! Instead of war, hatred, drugs, adultery, crime and violence, hunger, affliction, lust and lies, we need plenty of love, joy, honesty, peace, prosperity and justice for all," The angels smiled and said with simultaneity, "We cloth stock fruits — only seeds." We must plant seeds to have a marriage that will satisfy God and ourselves. God is willing and ready to help us. Are we willing to submit to God?

Dr. Wilferd A. Peterson has given us the secret of a good marriage. In "The Art of Marriage." he writes, A good marriage must be created. In the art of marriage, the little things are big things...

It is never being too old to hold hands.
It is remembering to say, "I love you" at least once each day.
It is never going to sleep angry.
It is having a mutual sense of values and common objectives.
It is standing together facing the world.
It is fanning a circle of love that gathers in the whole family.
It is speaking words of appreciation and demonstrating gratitude in thoughtful ways.
It is having the capacity to forgive and forget.
It is finding room for the things of the spirit.

It is a common search for the good and the beautiful. It is not only marrying the right partner, but it is being the right partner."

Dr. Peterson shared "The Art of Marriage" with his church First United Methodist Church in Montgomery, Alabama.

Dr. Karl K. Stegall, Pastor of First UMC at the time of this writing gave permission for this Printing, which appeared in the church bulletin, published February 14, 1999, Volume 6, Issue 7.

PRAYER: Almighty God, help us to always use words to heal and nor to hurt. Give new life to all men and women who want to live for you. Help all of us remember II Corinthians 5:10, "For we must all appear before the judgment seat of Christ, that each one may receive the things done in the body, according to what he has done, whether good or bad."

But you who are holy are the temple of the living God. And God said, "I will dwell in them and walk among them. I will be their God and they shall be my people" (llCor.7:6b).

MAN, LOVE YOUR WIFE AND SAVE YOUR LIFE!
WOMAN, LOVE YOUR HUSBAND AND SAVE YOUR LIFE!

WALKING in LOVE

SCRIPTURES: ROMANS 14:1-15:6; 1
CORINTHIANS 8 1 CORINTHIANS 13

Frederick Buechner in his book The Magnificent Defeat penned the following words:

"The love for equals is a human thing-of friends, brother for brother. It is to love what is loving and lovely. The world smiles.

The love for the less fortunate is a beautiful thing-the love for chose who suffer, for those who are poor, sick, the failures, the unlovely. This is compassion, and it touches the heart of the world.

The love for the more fortunate is a rare thing–to love those who succeed where we fail, to rejoice without envy with those who rejoice, the love of the poor for the rich, the rich for the poor, of the black man for the white man, the white man for the black man. The world is always bewildered by its saints.

And then there is the love for the enemy-for the one who does not love you but mocks, threatens, and inflicts pain. The tortured loves the torturer. This is God's love. It conquers the world. This is the Magnificent Defeat" (p. 105).

Love is the goal of the Christian life. Paul, an apostle, has some matchless passages on the meaning of love in his several letters. Students of the Bible call Paul's Holy Ghost-inspired ode to Christian love, a sonnet of love. Paul has Jesus Christ in mind. Our Lord is the epitome of Christian love. This is the message chat the Corinthians needed to hear, and it is the message that we need to continuously hear.

Starting with 1 Corinthians 12:31 and continuing through 1 Corinthians 13:13, Paul embarks on an extensive treatment of the superiority and supremacy of love over spiritual gifts. Without love, our spiritual gifts are useless. At the close of Chapter 12, Paul says, "But earnestly desire the best gifts. And yet I show you a more excellent way" (v.31). Paul was saying that you may be blessed with the spiritual gifts, but if you do not have agape (the love of God within your heart) your gifts are ineffective. You will be nothing but a religious noise.

How do we walk in love? First, lee us acknowledge that Paul is not describing "puppy love." He is describing the rarest kind of love in the world and out of the world. It is the supernatural love. It is part of our nature as Christians. We must demonstrate love in all we do and say. It is putting love into action. Do we really love? Are we building up our neighbors, our families, our friends and even those who persecute us? Jesus told Israel and He speaks to us this day with the same velocity, "The first of all the commandments is: 'Hear, O Israel, the Lord our God, the Lord is one, and you shall love the Lord your God with all your heart, with all your soul, with all your mind, and with all your heart, with all your strength.' This is the First commandment. "And the second, like it, is this: 'You shall love your neighbor as yourself.' There is no other commandment greater than these" (Mark 12:29-32).

Who is your neighbor? Jesus defined the neighbor by telling the story of the Good Samaritan (Luke 10:33-37). In reference to this parable, Howard Thurman in his prolific writings stated with sure artistry, and great Power chat Jesus depicted what happens when a man responds directly to human needs across the barriers of class, race, and condition.

Thurman said, "Every man is potentially every other man's neighbor" (Jesus and the Disinherit, p.89).

Dr. Marcin Luther King, Jr. went to Memphis, Tennessee, in support of the city's striking sanitation workers, who were the low men on the totem pole. Dr. King in his speech cited the Good Samaritan as his role model. He delivered his now universally famous "I've Been to the Mountaintop" speech at Bishop Charles Mason Temple on April 3, 1968. The next day, his life was snuffed out by an assassin's bullet. Dr. King lived and died while he walked in love for his fellow men. Another great man of God, one of whom I have had correspondence, tutelage and permission to use some of his materials within my studies, Dr. John Townsend, stated in his writing "A Call to Love (Townsend, Called to Love, July 30, 2006) that "Dr. King reminded his audience of humanities duties. And so the first question that the priest asked - the first question that the Levite asked was, 'If I stop to help this man, what will happen to me?' But then the Good Samaritan came by and he reversed the question: 'If I do not stop to help this man, what will happen to me.?" That's the question that's before us, now."

That is the altruistic question that motivated Dr. King's life and ultimate sacrifice, and it should motivate all who wish to love and serve others. Who is your neighbor? He or she who is in need is your neighbor. Dr. King did not have to become a martyr. He was born in the Black upper class, yet he renounced it. He even gave away the proceeds from his Nobel Peace Prize, opting to live in poverty. Dr. King was noted for his altruism.

In the 13th Chapter of First Corinthians, apostle Paul describes and extols (lifts up, praise lavishly) the quintessential (pure, undiluted essence, the highest essence) nature of Christian love. This love is over and beyond essential love. It is love's ability to love the unlovable, those who persecute us. In First Corinthians 13:7, Paul cites four characteristics of Christian love: It always protects. It always trusts, hoping for the best. Even in the face of persecution, Christian love always hopes for the best. Christian love always perseveres in face of opposition, empowering us to overcome our circumstances. Christian love overlooks faults; it refuses to see them through natural eyes. Love has spiritual eyes. We Christians love with our hearts, loving what the eyes despise. William Shakespeare put it like this:

> "In faith, I do not love thee with mine eyes,
> For they in thee a thousand errors note;
> But 'tis my heart that loves what they despise,
> Who in despite of view is pleased to dote."
> (Verses taken from Shakespeare Sonnet # 141, "The
> Sonnets" Edited by Rex Gibson. Cambridge University
> Press, 1998, New York, NY p.164)

Can you dote on the one your eyes despise? God loves us like this, even greater than this. Nothing can inhibit God's love, Jesus told us to love our enemies, "But I say to you who hear: Love your enemies, do good to those who hate you, bless those who curse you, and pray for those who spitefully use you . . . But love your enemies, do good, and lend hoping for nothing in return; and your reward will be great, and you will be sons of the Most High. For He is kind to the unthankful and evil. Therefore, be merciful) just as your Father also is merciful" (Luke 6:24-36, The New King James Version).

We must love the unlovable. I have a dear friend who works hard to help other people, especially children in need. She will volunteer to help them through purchases and utilizing systems that are available. She is a giving person. Yet, when we discuss loving those who do evil toward others, those who stand in the shoes of the enemy, she replies that she hasn't reached that level yet. She doesn't hate them, but she doesn't express love toward them either. Jesus said, "Love your enemies." Jesus had to apply that love to those who became His enemies, those who were of the household of Israel and He had to love those who weren't. God was our first love giver and His Son, Jesus, was a love-giver. He gave His life for us. In Luke Chapter 4, we are told that the opposition to the interpretation which Jesus was giving to the gospel of God increased. He was rejected at Nazareth. He then went down to Capernaum, a city of Galilee and was teaching them on the Sabbath. There He commanded unclean spirits to come out. They had to obey Him. He is Sovereign. Leaving the Synagogue and entering Simon's house, He found Simon's mother-in-law with fever. He stood over her and rebuked the fever, and it left her, and immediately she arose and served them (Luke 4:38-39). Jesus and His disciples withdrew from active work into semi-retirement around Tyre and Sidon. But, I am told that there was a woman, a Syrophoenician woman (Greek, referred to as a Gentile, or as some would say a "pagan"), who had an urgent request on behalf of her daughter. This woman broke into His retreat. Jesus knew who she was. He even had conversation with her. Some theologians said that Jesus was experiencing deep frustration and humiliation, but the woman was desperate and her voice touched Him and He said, "O woman great is your faith! Let it be to you as you desire. Go woman, go in peace, your faith hath saved you." And her daughter was healed from that very hour (Matthews 15:22-28; Mark 7:26). Jesus healed great multitudes. Faith attracts love, and loves attracts many blessings including healings.

Now, everyone didn't like what Jesus taught. On one occasion, while He was teaching in the Temple, the chief priest and the Pharisees sent temple officers to arrest Him. But they returned without Jesus, explaining, "No man spoke like this man!" (John 7:40-46).

Then Jesus applied His love to the Roman ruler, the enemy. Rome, the capital of the Roman Empire was wealthy, literary and artistic. The Romans worshiped many pagan gods. In 63 B.C, Palestine fell into the hands of the Romans. After this takeover, there was an increasing desecration of the Holy Land. In the midst of this political climate that was taking place, Jesus began His teaching and ministry. His words were directed to the House of Israel. He profoundly said to love your enemy so that you may be children of your Father who is in heaven. Rome was the enemy, symbolizing total frustration. But Jesus walked in love.

Christian love conquers all. Therefore, it does not delight in evil, wrong doing. Love is the more excellent way, and it finds its delight in the truth. This is a far cry from the way we behave toward others. Paul told the Romans, and he is telling us today not to think of ourselves more highly than we ought to think, but to think soberly, as God has dealt to each one a measure of faith (Romans 12:3).

Apostle Paul knew that it is human nature to feel superior to the weak, the poor, the failures, the captive, the helpless and the hopeless, and those who are different from us. Being an astute psychologist, he knew that we associate defeat with weakness and failure with wickedness. We think that we are strong and we are pure, we think, and we draw back from those who are obviously not qualified to keep company with us. Paul attacks our citadel of self-confidence with a question and a declaration. "Why do you pass judgment on your brother? Or you, why do you despise your brother? For we shall all stand before the judgment seat of God. So each of us shall give account of himself/ herself to Gods" (Romans 14:10ff). He knew that in the presence of God's perfect love and purity, all of us stand condemned; therefore, none has ground to feel superior to others.

As children of God, you most not think too lowly of yourselves either because you are a new creation; old things have passed away; behold, all things have become new (2 Car. 5:17). However, you have an old sinful nature and because of this sinful nature, some disregard the feeling of others. Now, when we do this, "we are no longer walking in love."

We Christians know that part of our duty in the pursuit of excellence in Christ is to find the right path for ourselves, but we are obliged also to help others find a determined path. We are never to put a stumbling block or any hindrance in the way of others. To walk in love requires us to show respect for others, control our attitudes, words, and actions toward ochers. If we are not doing this, we are not walking in love. Love for God is inextricably tied to love for others.

Paul urges his readers and hearers to "act from faith!" (14:23) For Paul, faith is a conscious relationship with God, a sense of living with the Divine, as companions in the way life should be lived. We know that faith is not a static state of mind, but a living awareness of responsibility to Christ and for our fellow human persons. When we Christians live in harmony with each other, our praise will not be discordant. We will all glorify the God and Father of our Lord Jesus Christ.

When we truly love one another, Paul contended, we would do everything in our power to strengthen others as we walk with them in the way of Christ. Paul was conscious of the need of Christians to leave no doubt in the mind of observers that the conduct characteristic of believers in Christ stood in sharp contrast with the behavior of the various idolatries chat were widely practiced in that era. Surely, the same is true today.

I challenge all of us to live righteously. The challenge is to love Jesus more than we love all else, to serve Him with all of our heart, mind and soul. And then we will walk in love. The 13th chapter of First Corinthians references us to true love. 1Corinthians 13:8 tells us that love never fails. Loving God and being loved by God should permeate all of one's life.

Roberta Bondi, contends in The Conversations with the Early Church----To Love as God Loves contends that our growing love is a continuous movement into God's love, as the ancient Christian writers say. But because God's love is without limit, and because being human means sharing in the image of God, we can never in our human loving reach the limit of our ability to love. This means that though we may love fully at any moment, it is not perfect love unless that loves continues to grow. (p.23)

Bondi says, being a Christian means learning to love with God's love. But God's love is not a warm feeling in the pit of the stomach. It has definite characteristics we learn in the course of our life, in the behavior and teaching of the early moments in time, as we ponder over what we can say about God as God deals with us, and finally, as we model our lives on what we have learned" (pp. 107-108).

Professor Bondi was one of my professors, also.

We must remember that God's love is uncompromising and unconditional. It never fails; it reaches out to everyone. God revealed this point when He sent His Son to the Cross to die for our sins. He knew that we were a rebellious people. To have a true encounter with this loving God will change the heart of humankind. Yes, the world needs plenty of love. Mere is a song out there that says, "What the world needs now is love, sweet love:1 We who are called to Christianity, and even those who do not know Christ must show that love is prominent in our lives. When we love one another, we walk in love. My second challenge to you is for you to study the life of Jesus, and you will find love, cherish love, grow in love and surely walk in love. The apostle Paul reaches the climax of his great teaching of love within 1 Corinthians 13 by saying, "There are three things that remain -faith, hope and love -and the greatest of these is love." God is love. Everybody needs love and to be loved! If you deny this fact, you are not being true to yourself. Let us accept agape love and walk in love. Agape love is the debt that we will never, never pay off. It does not matter how much we have; we are still under obligation to keep walking in love. The genuine love for others is the litmus test of true Christianity.

Tina Turner released a song tided, "What's Love Got to Do with It?" Tina called love "a second-hand emotion." Paul knew better, and we know better. Love has everything to do with it. We need agape love. We need love. After all, our Savior and Lord said, "A new commandment I give you, that you love one another; as I have loved you, that you also love one another. By this all will know that you are My disciples, if you have love for one another" (John 13: 34,35). Love is the hallmark of Christ's true disciples. Love is no second-hand emotion. "Love will never end." He who does not love does not know God, for God is love (1John 4:8). Love endures, it never fails. This statement is not true of the other gifts included in First Corinthians 13. All other gifts will cease. Yes, your gift of knowledge, which makes you look and feel powerful, will cease. But love and love only can make you grow to your full stature. However, we cannot practice love in isolation. If we truly have agape love, we will hold on to other essential principles in life such as faith in God, hope, holiness, wisdom, and obedience. Without these characteristics, we are out of the will of God. You must know that to love abundantly is to live abundantly, and to love forever is to live forever.

"For God so loved the world that He gave His only begotten Son that whoever believes in Him should not perish but have everlasting life" (John 3:16). I love You.

WHY PRAY? PRAYER CHANGES YOUR LIFE and YOUR CIRCUMSTANCES

SCRIPTURE: LUKE 18:1

Some of you are saying, 'June talks a lot about praying." I am tempted to respond with the story of the preacher, new to his congregation, who preached a mighty and powerful sermon on stealing and his congregation was very much moved by it. The next Sunday morning he preached the same sermon and they wondered about his preaching it. The third Sunday morning he preached the same message, once again. After the third time, a committee, members of the Administrative Council and the Worship Committee met, with him. They asked him if he had some other messages because they were tired of the same old sermon. His response was, "Yes, I have many." They followed his response with, "TI1en, how long are you going to preach on stealing?" He replied, "I am going to preach on stealing until you stop stealing, and When if you stop, I will change my message."

I am not attempting to give the same message on prayer, but I do plan to preach on prayer at various intervals until we are known as a praying church.

E.Stanley Jones said, "Prayer is surrender-surrender to the will of God and cooperation with chat will. If I throw out a boathook from the boat and catch hold of the shore and pull, do I pull the shore to me, or do I pull myself to the shore? Prayer is not pulling God to my will, but the aligning of my will to the will of God." p.73.

Prayer is an offering up of our desires unto God for things agreeable to His will, in the name of Jesus the Christ, with confession of our sins, and thankful acknowledgement of His mercies.

The question is, "Do you really believe in prayer?" It is relatively easy to discuss prayer, but unless we have experienced the power of prayer, it is but a powerless expression of hidden desire. Until we as Christians become aware of the unlimited power which God has encrusted to us, we shall not be able to do much in the saving of ourselves, our families, our communities, our world. I know that prayer makes a difference. My prayer partner and I have had prayer every morning over the telephone for more than twenty years. We have seen miracles that God has worked in many areas. We have seen God not moving in some areas, but that did not stop us, for we know God's timing is the right timing, not ours. Therefore, we keep the faith because the prayers are to bless someone, and our God is in the blessing business. I have been personally heated through prayer. My daughter, who was very ill, and the doctors were concerned as to whether she would make it through one night after a serious operation, was healed through prayer. In addition to the problem of our concern, through the many prayers sent up, several other conditions she experienced were healed. God answers prayer. A requirement to getting your prayer answered is your belief. Actually, the healing comes from within. That is the way we are made. If you want any prayer answered that will glorify God, speak the healing words. Jesus came chat we may have life and have it abundantly.

J. K.Johnston in his book Why Christians Sin cells a tale about a small town chat had historically been "dry," but then a local businessman decided to build a tavern. A group of Christians from a local church were concerned and planned an all-night prayer meeting to ask God to intervene. It just so happened that shortly thereafter lighting struck the bar and it burned to the ground. The owner of the bar sued the church, claiming that the prayers of the congregation were responsible, but the church hired a lawyer to argue in court that they were not responsible. The presiding judge, after his initial review of the case, seated, "No matter how this case comes out, one thing is clear. The tavern owner believes in prayer and the Christians do not."

I read that in its early days, Dallas Theological Seminary was in critical need of $10,000 to keep the work going. During a prayer meeting, renowned

Bible teacher Harry Ironside, a lecturer at the school, prayed, "Lord, you own the cattle on a thousand hills. Please sell some of your cattle to help us meet this need." Shortly after the prayer, a check for $10,000 arrived at the school, sent days earlier by a friend who had no idea of the urgent need or of Ironside's prayer. The man simply said the money came from the sale of some of his cattle! On a smaller scale, I needed $400.00 more than I had saved for graduation at Florida State University. I had no one to call upon for the money. I was working, but rent and other bills did not allow me to have one penny to apply to this need. Now, no one knew that I needed it either, except God. I prayed and asked God for the four hundred dollars knowing that God owns all of the money in the world. A few days later, I went to my mailbox and pulled out the junk mail, which covered a letter from a group of ladies in the exact amount of $400.00. Immediately, I thanked God for it. I had already thanked Him prior to my receiving it, I know He hears and answers prayers. Most recently, a friend of mine---a sister in Christ, had a tavern across the street from her church. She invited the frequent visitors to church. She never confessed that she prayed for the tavern to close, yet I have my beliefs. The tavern owner closed the facility and gave her the first opportunity to purchase it. It is torn down, The tavern is no longer in existence and the property will be used to glorify God.

Do you really believe in prayer? Do you pray? I have heard people say, "Why pray, God knows our needs?" We must pray because Jesus told us to ask and it shall be given. Jesus taught His disciples to pray. We must clearly and precisely ask what we need from God and thank Him for answering our prayers.

The famed C. H. Spurgeon once said: "There is no need for us to go beating about the bush, and not telling the Lord distinctly what it is that we crave at His hands. Nor will it be seemly for us to make any attempt to use fine language; but let us ask God in the simplest and most direct manner for just the things we want...I believe in business prayers. I mean prayers in which you take to God one of the many promises which He has given us in His Work, and expect it to be fulfilled as certainly as we look for the money to be given when we go to the bank and cash a check.... Tell the clerk what form we wish to take the amount, count the cash, and then go our way to attend to other business. This is just an illustration of the method in which we should draw supplies from the Bank of Heaven" (The Kneeling Christian Clarion Classic, 1986, pp.79-80).

Jesus speaks to us through Matthew 18 verses 19, 20. "Again I say to you, if two of you agree on earth concerning anything that they ask, it will be done for them by My Father in heaven. For where two or three are gathered in my name, there am I in the midst of them." In John 14 verses 12, 14, Jesus gives us words of assurance that our prayers are answered.

Prayer has great power, great authority. For Moses, prayer divided the Red Sea and rolled up flowing rivers, turned clear water into blood. For Elijah, prayer quenched flames of fire. For Daniel it bound the mouth of lions. For Paul, it disarmed vipers and poison. TIle Bible tells us that prayer stopped the course of the moon and arrested the sun in its race across the sky. It has burst open iron gates and set the prisoners free. Prayer recalled souls from eternity. It conquered the strongest devils and commanded legions of angels down from heaven.

Prayer has brought one man from the belly of a big fish and carried another in a chariot of fire to heaven. Prayer is an awesome, mighty force in this world, today. In Matthew 18, we have three very illuminating insights into prayer, from the greatest authority in the world, Jesus. We see that prayer is an authority operating in mystery. When He talks about binding and loosing, our Lord is saying that it is possible for ordinary people like you and me to exercise extraordinary power, chat heaven would in some sense ratify what is done on earth; chat we would be put in couch with a world beyond the world that is visible to our senses. This is what He means by contrasting heaven with earth. Take these words seriously. This is real.

WHAT DOES PRAYER DO?

Prayer reaches up, up to God. Prayer is communion with God: it is the soul in fellowship with its Maker. Prayer is adoration. It is more than a petition, more than mere asking, it is communion. It is the soul coming home to its natural habitat ---God. When prayer reaches up, the answering hand of God reaches down and the two meet. If prayer can bring the soul of a person up into the presence of God, then prayer has power. And it can! The psalmist cries out, "My soul thirsts...for the living God" Psalm 42:2). It is in and through prayer that we discover that a new spiritual awareness.

Prayer reaches in. The soul finds God through prayer finds itself. No person knows himself until he or she finds God. When we pray, we see ourselves as God sees us, for prayer is the mirror of the soul. Tell me what you pray for, I can tell you the kind of person you are. You can discover more about yourself, your weaknesses, and your frailties through the power of prayer than by all the courses you may take in psychology, self-analysis or anything else.

Prayer reaches through. The soul first finds God, then itself, and then its neighbors. Prayer reaches its greatest privilege and joy when it becomes intercessory prayer. The more you pray for other people and the less you pray for yourself, the better things go. Try scattering good will, love and prayers all around, everywhere, and you will be astonished not only by what it does for other people but also by how it comes back to you in generous abundance. We read in the Bible, "Cast thy bread upon the waters, for you will find it after many days" (Ecclesiastes: 11:I). Cast your prayers upon people and just see how they come back to you. Pray for other people, for those who don't like you. Pray for those in need, those who are in authority; and those who are miserable, jealous, pray for them anyway. Bless them. Do your best. Do your part. Pray and pray and pray. If you don't like someone, pray that God will change your heart. A Christian ought to always pray. We don't know why God waits till Christians pray before He begins to do what He has intended all along, and even announced that He would do it, but that is what He does. Read all about it in Daniel. Men read about it in James 4:2. James said, "You have not I because you ask not." God waits until we ask before He moves. Scripture states that God will neither hear us nor look upon us as we pray, if we are regarding iniquity in our hearts or retaining any known and unconfessed sins (Is. 59:1-2). It is imperative that we ask God to forgive us prior to making our request. God forgives. Read Isaiah 43:25: "I, even I, am He who blots out your transgressions for my own sakes; And I will not remember your sins."

There is nothing that needs to have dominion over us; "Sin has no dominion over us." Paul said, "For you are not under the law but under grace" (Rom.6:14). Jude tells us that we should pray in the spirit Jude 20). Why? The Holy Spirit assists in prayer. We are to be guided and controlled by the One that dwells in us. We need the Spirit's guidance to know what to pray. We need the Spirit's mind to pray unselfishly, purely, and correctly. We need the Spirit's intercession so that we may pray according to the will of God. Christ, always filled with the Holy Spirit, prayed, "Nevertheless not my will, but yours, be done." Let us become Christ-Centered and pray. Don't forget to pray for those who spitefully use you and persecute you (Matthew 5:44). They need a close walk with God. Pray and if you need to repent, repent and pray!

Paul Harvey told about a three-year old boy who went to the grocery store with his mother. Before they entered the store, she had certain instructions for the little boy: "Now you're not going to get any chocolate chip cookies, so don't even ask." She put him in the child's seat, and off they went- up and down the aisles. He was doing fine until they came to the cookie section. Seeing the chocolate chip cookies, he said, "Mom, can I have some chocolate chip cookies?" She said, "I told you not even to ask. You're not going to get any at all." They continued down the aisles, but in the search for certain items she had to back track, and they ended up in the cookie aisle again. "Mom, can I please have some chocolate cookies?" She said, "I told you that you can't have any; now sit down and be quiet."

Finally, they arrived at the checkout counter. The little boy sensed that the end was in sight, that this might be his last chance. He stood up on the seat and shouted in his loudest voice, "In the name of Jesus, may I have some chocolate chip cookies?" Everyone in the checkout lanes laughed and applauded. Do you think the little boy got his cookies? You bet! The other shoppers moved by anguish and grief." Eli answered, "Go in peace, and may the God of Israel grant you what you have asked of Him" (1 Samuel 1:17). Then she went away and ate something, and her face was no longer downcast. So in the course of time Hannah conceived and gave birth to a son. She called him Samuel, saying, "Because I asked the Lord for him" (1 Samuel 1:2P28). Like Hannah, we are tested so that our character will match our dreams. The phenomenal women know this to be true.

Second, to become phenomenal, we must be willing to make sacrifices. Esther, another great woman of the Bible, exemplifies what it means to be a phenomenal woman. She moves from concern for pure expedience to radical obedience. The story is familiar to us. Through the strategizing of Mordecai, her cousin and adoptive father, Esther found herself in the position of Queen. When suddenly I-Taman's plan to destroy the Jews was made known, Mordecai proceeded to instruct Esther by messenger of her responsibility as a Jew. Here, I would like to focus on Esther's obedience; let's call it faithful resistance. Esther had two opportunities for obedience. The first was in Mordecai's initial plan to conceal her heritage and for her to "be a candidate" for the position of queen. Esther accepted this challenge with little or no resistance. The second plan was risky. Esther was being called upon to stand up for the oppressed. Jews. This identification as a Jew and the fact that she was a woman made it doubly risky. After fasting and praying, Esther approached the King and saved her people from destruction. In spite of the positive result, Esther's obedience in the second instance was a struggle. It required wrestling with what was at stake, primarily her life and personal security. Obedience here was not ordinary; it was faithful resistance and radical obedience. This story affords us the opportunity to reflect upon the relationship between the personal and the political, the private and the public, the individual and the community. Esther's decision to reveal her identity was one that had a direct impact on the whole Jewish community. Only when Esther had succeeded in extricating herself from personal concerns was she free co affirm her real connection to her people and her real purpose in life. Risking it all in faithful resistance to the oppressive and debilitating structures may mean losing privileged positions. It may cost you a promotion. It may cost, but sisters and brothers, on the other hand, it may save your life and the lives of your loved ones. As a phenomenal person you will speak words of comfort, encouragement, love, words of defense for the helpless, the slandered, and the judged. As a phenomenal person, you will speak words of confrontation for chose whose sharp tongues spew sarcasm, lies and condemnation. To be a phenomenal person, you will speak words of anger to those who gain their own wealth or power at the expense of others, words of reconciliation for those who have been hurt. Often, we know the words of God that fill our mouths, but we fear or refuse to speak them. Risking it all means having the audacity to speak out and empower other people. Camille Cosby said, "When we empower one another we are disempowering those who certainly will not empower us, and history should have caught us this, long ago."

The records of Phenomenal Women such as Sojourner Truth, who spoke out fearlessly against racism and sexism, and Jarena Lee, who preached when the church said she could not preach, have inspired many women to venture into fields that were closed to us. As I write, we have some ministers and some women saying, "Women should not preach." God will use whomever God wants to do what God wants done. Many of our ancestors have been inspired to use their God--given talents in spite of hardship and having done so, they became phenomenal women. Maya Angelou captured that equation in the poems that she pens. Her basic theme is "the refusal of the human spirit to be hardened and the persistence of innocence against all obstacles."

CAN'T YOU HEAR THESE PHENOMENAL WOMEN SAYING:

"Out of the huts of history's shame, I rise
Up from a past that's rooted in pain, I rise
I'm a black ocean; leaping and wide, welling and swelling
I bear in the tide.
Leaving behind nights of horror and fear, I rise
Into a daybreak that's wondrously clear, I rise"

(The line above was taken from Maya Angelou's poem "And Still I Rise")
Permit me to name a few other women that I consider to be or have been Phenomenal Women. Space will allow me to name only a few. I realize there are so many more.

Mother Theresa, who gave her life helping the indigent, impoverished people

Mrs. Rosa Parks, Mother of the Civil Rights Movement Dr. Gloria Randle Scott, President of Bennett College

Dr. Mae Jennison, The First Black Woman in Space

Dr. Mary Frances Berry, Education and Child Rights Advocate

Congress woman Corrine Brown and Congress woman Carrie Meeks (my former teacher), from Florida

Virginia Hamilton, America's most honored writer of books for children

Kathy Clark, Theologian, Editor, Organizer

Teresa Frye, Theologian at Candler School of Theology Ruth Monroe, Executive Administrator of Bahamian

Ministries

Ellen Johnson Sirleaf President of Liberia, Africa

Dr. Trudie Reed, President of Bethune-Cookman University

Many women pastors, ministers, evangelists, prophetesses, and my Christian sisters within my hometown are phenomenal. And the list goes on and on and on, not to be exhaustive. These women and others heard the call and answered the call. But you have heard a call as well. I challenge you who are young, middle aged, or elderly to answer your call. God is not through with you yet. You still have work to do for Him. I often hear the elderly say, "I can't do that, or I am just too old." Do you know that age is not a deterrent with God-inspired people? God uses women and men of age to gee His work done. I will name a few:

Golda Meir became Prime Minister of Israel when she was 71.

Mathematician Mary Fairfax Somerville published On Molecular and Microscopic Science when she was 89.

Estela De Carlotto at the age of 69 was president of the Abuelas. She worked with human rights organizations in Argentina and has helped many people.

The Roman Statesman Cato began to study Greek when he was 80.

A man graduated from college in May 1999 at the age of 94. He planned to work coward his master's and doctorate degrees.

Evie Marshall Hall, used by God on many occasions to

prophesy, quilt maker and educator, is writer at the age of 97. Her column appears in the Selma Times Journal, monthly.

God doesn't have retirees. And I would be remiss if I didn't speak of those phenomenal women in the workplace, within the home (domestic engineers), and those who need to yet be recognized. God would have all of us to have faith in Him. Our major problem, however, is our self-centeredness. We think we have accomplished the assignments given to us within our own power and with our current resources. We have forgotten that when God speaks, He always reveals what He is going to do, not what He wants us to do for Him. We must surrender to Him, so that He can do His work through us. With our limited abilities, resources and faith, we can proceed confidently and accomplish any task God has anointed us to do. God knows that He is going to bring to pass what He purposes. God wants to reveal Himself to a watching, hurting, fearful world: Therefore, He will ask us to be involved with Him in a God-size assignment. When we are confronted with such a great assignment, many times we will face a crisis of belief. If we are sure that we have heard His voice and not the voice of the stranger, we have nothing to fear. The stranger does not want us to do God's work.

Women, it is critically important that we as women believe that we are created in the image of God and that we are wonderfully made. Philippians 4:13 tells us that we can do all things through Christ who strengthens us. Receive the Word and believe the Word. Now, go and do the work God has assigned you to do. You are a phenomenal woman! You are a phenomenal person!

WHAT IF GOD HAD AN ANSWERING MACHINE

SCRIPTURE: CALL ON ME AND I WILL ANSWER
THEE... SAID THE LORD. JEREMIAH 33:3

Margie was a good friend of mine attending Candler School of Theology during my tenure there. She asked me to call her one Saturday morning. We talked the night before and she was not feeling well. In fact, she was ill. Margie and I lived in different counties. Responding to her request, I called her at approximately eight o'clock that Saturday morning. She did not answer her phone. After several attempts of trying to reach her, I called 911. I expected to talk to an operator. Instead, a recording answered the phone. I was placed on hold. Every few minutes, the recording would say, "Your call is very important to us, do not hang up. The next available representative will answer your call." At this point I asked myself, "What if God had an answering machine?"

After having received four or five of these messages, I was just about to hang up when I heard an operator say, "May I help you, please?" I told her the nature of my call and the urgency of someone checking on Margie. I gave her the name of the county, Margie's address, phone number and all of the details. The request was reasonable, and the operator told me that she would have an officer to visit Margie's residence. And then I was in for another long wait. After waiting in anxiety for approximately 40 minutes, I called 911 again. Would you believe that I was put on hold again? When the operator answered my call, she stated that an officer had investigated and all seemed to be in place. She said that the officer didn't talk with Margie but a neighbor had seen her. I was relieved.

I know that the city is large, but I was surprised and frustrated chat 911 placed me on hold for long periods of time, twice. I thank God that my call was not really an emergency. Aren't you glad that we serve a God who doesn't have an answering machine? We have learned to live with answering machines as a necessary part of modernization. But I have wondered, "What if God decides to install an automated answering machine? What if God used the familiar excuse "All of the angels are helping other customers right now; your call is important; please stay on the line. Your call will be answered in the order in which it was received."

Can you imagine getting these kinds of responses as you call

on God in prayer? Do you know your party's extension? Press O for the directory.

If you would like to speak to Gabriel, press 1.

For Michael, press 2.

For any other angel, press 3.

If you want King David to sing a Psalm to quiet your nerves, press 4.

If you want to speak to a Prophet, press 5.

For all other questions, press 6.

If you need FAITH and want to speak to Abraham, press 7.

For answers to questions about yourself, just trust me.

OR

Our computers show that you have called once today, already. Please hang up and give someone else a turn.

OR

This office is closed for the weekend. Our office hours are Monday through Friday from 8:00 a.m. to 5:00 p.m.

Thank God for not having an answering machine. God said to the Prophet Jeremiah, "Call on me and I will answer thee and will tell thee great and mighty things that you have not known" Jeremiah 33:3). Truly, this passage speaks to the healing of Israel after the punishment. Now this is God speaking and my Bible tells me that God is the same God, yesterday, today and forever (Hebrews 13:8). He is telling us to call upon Him, seek Him today.

Thank God, you cannot call Him too often! You only need co ring once and God hears you. Because of Jesus, you will never get a busy signal. God takes each call and knows the caller, personally. He even knows the nature of the call and has already answered before you called. We serve an Almighty God. Isaiah tells us, "Then you will call, and the Lord will answer; you will cry for help and He will say, 'Here I am.'"(Isaiah 58:9). Thank Him before you see the manifestation of your prayers. God will show us great and wonderful things, if only we believe!

The Reverend Richard L. Sheffield used this illustration in one of his sermons. He said, "In a 'Dennis the Menace" comic in the Lima News, Dennis' line to this mother is "Before I tell you what happened, remember I'm just a little kid." My line to you is "Before I tell you about Jeremiah, remember I'm just a messenger.

Jeremiah, the prophet of God, was just a messenger. Jeremiah said to God, "I don't know what to say." God said, "I'll tell you what to say!" And what God said is what Jeremiah said.

Jeremiah was a Late Seventh-Early Sixth Century Prophet. He was the son of Hilkiah, a priest in the territory of Benjamin. I am told that Jeremiah received his Call and Commission from God in the 13th year of King Josiah (627 B.C.E.) and he was active in this king's reign.

What amazes me about the Prophets of the Old Testament is that even if they didn't see why God called them, they answered the call. Sometimes with excuses, but they answered. In the First Chapter — Jeremiah said, "Now the word of the Lord came to me saying, 'Before I formed you in the womb, I knew you; before you were born I sanctified you; I ordained you a prophet to the nations' (Jeremiah 1:4,5). Jeremiah received His commission from God not man but God.

Friends, don't you know that God knew you in your mother's womb? Do you desire to serve the Lord in a special ministry, and the door is closed? Do not try to force it open. Learn to wait on the Lord, and He will direct your path (Proverbs 3:5,6). Has God spoken to you? Are we like Jeremiah when we hear Him speak? Do we find excuses or objections in doing what God would have us do?

Jeremiah said, "Ah, Lord God! Truly I do not know how to speak, for I am a youth" (Jeremiah 1:6). This echoes the call of another prophet the lad Samuel (1 Samuel 1:3). Jeremiah continued but the Lord said to me: "Do not say, 'I am a youth,' For you shall go to all whom I send you, And whatever I command you, you shall speak. Do not be afraid of their faces, for I am with you to deliver you, says the Lord (Jeremiah 1:7,8). THIS IS THE REASSURANCE JEREMIAH RECEIVED FROM GOD. Sometimes, we, too, need that Blessed Assurance.

But God didn't leave Jeremiah there. God promised God's presence and aid in the face of persecution. He said, "Do not be afraid of them; for I am with you to deliver you'(1:8). Then the Lord put out his hand and touched Jeremiah's mouth and the Lord said to him, "Now I have put my words in your mouth"(1:9). God touched and placed divine words in the mouth of His prophets and He is doing the same thing, today.

Jeremiah was a prophet and Jeremiah called upon the God. During Jeremiah's time, there were always battles, and it was suspected that Babylon was the enemy from the north that would bring destruction to Judah in the south. Before coming to Jerusalem and before King's Josiah's death, the prophet preached both repentance by returning to the ancestral faith and acquiescence to the Babylonians as the sole means of avoiding national destructions. God is concerned about Nations. In fact, Jesus is coming back to judge the Nations. He will judge the individuals in the Nations. Although

Jeremiah was persecuted, he had hope in God. He preached that obedience to the commandments and to the covenant of Moses—not temple worship was Judah's only survival. To show his hope, his faith and his belief in God, Jeremiah went out and purchased land, for he knew God would deliver. We need to call on the Lord in every situation of our lives. In good times, call on the Lord and in difficult times call upon the Lord. If you need a miracle, call upon the Lord. When in pain, call upon the Lord. He told us to cast our care upon Him and He will sustain us (Psalms 55:22).1 Peter 1:4 tells us, "He has given us His great and precious promises: Call upon the Lord! God doesn't have an answering machine. He hears and answers our calls. After having called upon Him, give God thanks for all He has done. Pray that His will is done in your life! Not your will, but God's will. He knows what is best for all of us. For God said, "Call on me and I will answer thee...God doesn't have an answering machine nor does He have anyone accepting His calls. Try Him! Call upon Him! God hears and answers our call. Many times, I felt that I was rejected, left alone, humiliated, but I called on the Lord and my -- God heard my call and answered my prayers. Glory be to the King of Kings! My challenge to you is called upon the Lord! Note: Margie lived in Nashville, Tennessee. I preached this sermon as Margie sat in the audience of St. Paul United Methodist Church during her visit to Pensacola. After church, she said, "I could feel the Spirit of God within that sermon." Now Margie is at rest, but her work, especially with children, lives on.

JESUS BLESSES THE LITTLE CHILDREN

SCRIPTURE: MATTHEW 19:13,14

Some time ago, Bishop Neal Luckett challenged the United Methodist Council of Bishops by telling them to think back to when they were children and then answer the following questions: Do you remember what happened when you became ill or had a dental problem? Were you ever really hungry or had to go hours — maybe days — without proper food or perhaps without any food? What did you do? What did the adults in your life or around you do for you?

We may have never experienced the dilemma of hunger or a lack of medical care, but many children have and are still experiencing such things. Within the book of Matthew 19:13 - 14, Jesus blesses the little children. The scripture says "Then the little children were brought to Him that He might put His hands on them and pray, but the disciples rebuked them. Jesus said, "Let the little children come to me, and do not forbid them; for such is the kingdom of heaven."

The plight of children and the impoverished raises critical theological concerns. Many churches are evaluating this great concern. The United Methodist Church is challenged to evaluate this concern on the basis of its theological grounding, the Wesleyan heritage, and its mission in this world. God has called the Church to a higher level of dedication and commitment on behalf of children, As a result, the Methodists caught the vision for the Children's Homes, which was established in 1890. The question is, "Are the churches doing their fair share in supporting the Children's Home (yes, many are, but some are not), or are the adults too busy doing their own thing and forgetting the future generation?"

Historically, Methodism was born among the impoverished of the eighteenth century in England. In my research, I found studies that document that the poor were the focus of the early Methodist Movement. John Wesley, the founder, was especially concerned that impoverished children learn not only to write, to read and cast accounts, but also more especially (by God's assistance), to know God and Jesus Christ whom He had sent. Methodist preachers were expected to spend time with children. If any retaliated, Wesley's response was, "Gift or no gift, you are to do it, else you are not called to be a Methodist preacher." Wesley's commitment to children and the impoverished went beyond friendship and proclamation. He provided holistically for their needs. He provided education/ opened free clinics and the list goes on and on. I am told that in the eighteenth century, Methodism was a movement of the poor) by the poor and for the poor; and Wesley considered affluence to be the most serious threat to the continued vitality and faithfulness of the Methodist Movement. Wesley was convinced that the poor are a means of grace. He said, "We must bless the poor, help the poor° For God blesses those who bless the poor." Psalm 41:1 - 3 informs us, "Happy are those who consider the poor; the Lord delivers them in the day of trouble. The Lord protects them and keeps them alive: they are called happy in the land. He will not give them up to the will of their enemies. The Lord sustains them on their sickbed; in their illness He heals all their infirmities."

The churches in the United Methodism have experienced an alarming loss of not only impoverished but middle-class children, as well. This loss has occurred at a time when children are increasingly at risk physically, mentally, and spiritually. Really, we are all at risk. One great theologian asked whether there is a judgment upon the Church that calls for immediate action. Mr. Wesley's feared that because of the affluence of the Church, it was separating itself from the impoverished, having the form of religion but lacking its power.

A church separated from "the least of these" is separated from the source of its identity and power, and the God who is among the most vulnerable. The children and the impoverished, therefore, are a means by which God restores and brings life. God is in solidarity with the most vulnerable. Are we? What would Jesus say to adults in the United States today relative to our children? Did you know that more than fifteen million American children live in poverty? There were nine million children without basic health care a few years ago, Surely the numbers have increased as I write. Millions die of hunger because there is no food, for them. Millions are killed because of senseless violence, and millions suffer because of abuse or neglect.

I stated that the plight of children and the impoverished raise critical theological concerns. The apostle Paul confronts us with the basic challenge: "Therefore, be imitators of God, as beloved children, and live in love, as Christ loved us" (Eph. 5:1). The Church is called upon to imitate and be a sign of the presence of the God revealed in the Scriptures and supremely in Jesus Christ. Faithfulness to God requires solidarity with and justice for the most vulnerable. Who are the most vulnerable? They are the widows, orphans, the children, and the poor. Psalm 82 verses 3 and 4 read as follows: "Defend the poor and fatherless;

Do justice to the afflicted and needy. Deliver the poor and needy; free them from the hand of the wicked." Another version of this scripture says, "Give justice to the weak and orphan, and maintain the rights of the lowly and the destitute. Rescue the weak and the needy, deliver them from the hand of the wicked." It does not matter which version we read, we are to get off our high horses and help God's children.

Matthew 25:35-40 tell us that Jesus so closely identified with the poor and the "least of these" that ministry done unto them is done unto Him. That's why we need to make a sacrifice and contributor to those in need. I wouldn't ask you to do anything that I wouldn't do. Let me ask you — are you ministering unto God? The Gospels identify the reign of God with children. Mark's gospel says, "Then he took a little child and set him in the midst of them. And when He had taken him in His arms, He said to them. "Whoever receives one of these little children in My name receives Me; and whoever receives Me, receives not Me but Him who sent Me.' (Mark 9:36-37).

In conclusion, Church, we are challenged by God Himself to respond to the crisis among the world's children and the impoverished people. We know that children are amazingly resilient. In order for this resiliency to manifest itself, we must provide a supportive community with hope and love and loving relationships, and sustain a value system necessary for children to flourish and fulfill their God-- given potential.

Every child needs to feel loved and wanted, and to have his or her basic needs provided. God has placed each of us in a preferred position. We have the opportunity to make a difference in the life of a child. We can make a difference, some do make a difference, and others must become actively involved in assuring that unfortunate children are cared for.

It is my prayer that each of us will give with great generosity during this third millennium to bless others. May Almighty God bless you greatly and multiply your giving as you bless others. In Jesus' name. Amen.

GOD CHOSE POWERLESS PEOPLE FOR POWERFUL TASKS

**SUBTITLE: NOT ONE HELD A PH.D, ED.D
or ANY OTHER DEGREE**

SCRIPTURE: 1 PETER 1:1; ACTS 4:13; JONAH 1-4

Peter identifies himself as a bond servant, an apostle of Jesus Christ. The apostle Peter is an example of how God used an ordinary, powerless man to advance His Kingdom. Peter was a fisherman. He was not a physician like Luke. He never had any rabbinical training. He knew how to fish, Peter was called by Jesus while engaged in his fisherman trade in Bethsaida on the Sea of Galilee. Acts 4:13 informs us, "Now when they (the Sanhedrin, "Rulers of the people and elders of Israel" as addressed by Peter) saw the boldness of Peter and John, and perceived that they were uneducated and untrained men, they marveled. And they realized that they had been with Jesus." The Greek language implies that Peter was ignorant and illiterate. However, we learned that 1 Peter is written in excellent Greek. We are told in 1 Peter 5:12, "By Silvanus, our faithful brother as I consider him, I have written you briefly, exhorting and testifying that this is the true grace of God in which you stand." So Peter had help. All of us need help. Joseph Nigro said in his writing, The Ordinary Person That God Uses, "God used Peter, a fisherman through the instruction of Jesus' three-year earthly ministry, the crystallization of Peter's commitment during the forty days of Jesus' pose-resurrection appearance, and through the coming of the Holy Spirit at Pentecost, to become a pillar of the New Testament Church" (Petros, a rock).

The question is, "Are you ready to do God's work?" My God looks for powerless people, ordinary people, and calls them to work for Him. Many times these people are ready. Other times these people are not ready. Most of us run and hide. Let's look at Jonah. Jonah was given a task to cake the gospel to the worst of the offenders at a given time. Assyria, a great, but evil empire, was Israel's most dreaded enemy. The Assyrians flaunted their power before God and the world through numerous acts of heartless cruelty. So when Jonah heard God tell him to go to Assyria and call the people to repentance, he ran in the opposite direction. But God stopped him and turned him around. Jonah's story is evidence of God's mercy and grace. No one deserved God's favor less than the people of Nineveh. Jonah knew this. But he knew that God would forgive and bless them if they turned from their sin and worshipped Him. He also knew the power of God's message. Jonah disliked the Assyrians and he wanted vengeance, not mercy, and so he ran. How many of us know that God wants us to do something and we are running? How many of us feel that we are just not ready or we can't do it? Well, we cannot in our own power, but with the power of God working within us we can do whatever we are assigned to do. Eventually, Jonah obeyed and preached in the streets of Nineveh and the people repented and were delivered from judgment. But 1 this did not satisfy Jonah; he sulked and complained to God.

> Jonah said, "Thar's why I ran away to Tarshish. I knew
> you were a gracious God, merciful, slow to anger, full of
> kindness; I knew how easily you could cancel your plans
> for destroying these people" (Jonah 4:2b).

And God had to confront Jonah about his self-centered values and lack of compassion. We must learn from this story of this reluctant prophet and determine to obey God, doing whatever He wants us to do whenever He wants it. Within the book of Jonah, God illustrates His love and concern for Gentiles even during the rime of the favorable relationship the children of Israel had with God. God reaches out to the entire world through His son Jesus.

God's grace extends to all who are willing to repent of their sins and commit to Him. David repented after committing adultery and having Bathsheba's husband killed (2 Samuel 12:-l-13a).

Abraham, known as Abram, treatment of Hagar was abusive. He also lied and said that Sarah was his sister (Genesis 12:13). This action showed distrust. After he repented, God called Abraham a friend of God, and Abraham was made the father of the Jewish race through whom all the families of the earth are blessed.

Samson had a sexual problem. He cried out to God and God heard his cry. He was anointed and, as Joseph A. Nigro said, "Brought the house down!"

God forgives sins. I could name many others who repented of their sins and were greatly used by God. 1 John 1:9 says, "If we confess our sins, He is faithful and just to forgive us our sins and to cleanse us from all unrighteousness." Philippians 1:6 tells us, "He who has begun a good work in you will complete it until the Until of Jesus Christ." Most willing to do the work of God was Mary. Until Gabriel's unexpected visit, Mary's life was going about as Well as she could hope. She had recently become engaged to a local carpenter, Joseph, and was anticipating married life to be like that of any ordinary person. But Mary's life was to become everything but ordinary. Angels don't usually make appointments to visit. As if Mary were being congratulated as the grand winner of a contest she had never entered, Mary found the angel's greeting puzzling and his presence frightening. What she heard next was the news almost every woman in Israel hoped to hear that her child would be the Messiah, God's promised Savior. Mary didn't doubt the message, but rather asked how her pregnancy would be possible.

Gabriel told her that the baby would be God's Son. Mary's reply to this was one that God has been waiting, in vain, to hear from so many other people. "I am the Lord's servant, and I am willing to do whatever he wants" (Luke 1:38). Lacer her song of joy to Elizabeth shows us how well she knew God, for her thoughts were filled with words from the Old Testament. God looks for powerless people to do great works for Him.

Jesus looks for powerless people to do great works in His name, as well.

He does not look for impressive resumes. When those of us who have been or are presently in a position to hire a worker, we usually select persons with the top resumes co interview.

Cecil Osborne's article in Yokefellows Newsletter a decade ago captured this phenomenon as he wrote the following: A little known firm which specializes in analyzing candidates for management positions in various organizations recently uncovered some old files which throw some interesting light on what some might consider essential skills and abilities for Christian service.

The report reads:

To: Jesus, son of Joseph
Regarding: 12 candidates for management positions

Dear Sir:

Thank you for submitting the resumes of the 12 men you have picked for positions in your new organization. All of them al have now taken our battery of tests, and we have not only run the results through our computer but also arranged personal interviews with each of them with our psychologist and vocational aptitude consultants.

It is our staff's opinion that most of your nominees are lacking in background, education and vocational aptitude for the type of enterprise you are undertaking. They do not have the team concept. We would recommend that you continue your search for persons of experience in managerial ability and proven capability.

Simon Peter is emotionally unstable and given to fits of temper. Andrew has absolutely no qualities of leadership. The two brothers, John and James, place personal interest above company loyalty. Thomas demonstrates a questioning attitude that would tend to undermine morale. We feel that it is our duty to tell you that The Greater Jerusalem Better Business Bureau has blacklisted Matthew. James, the son of Alphaeus, and 'Thaddeus, his friend, definitely have radical leanings, and they both register a high score on the manic scale. One of the candidates, however, shows a great potential. He is a man of ability and resourcefulness, meets people well, has a keen business mind and has contacts in high places. He is highly motivated, ambitious and responsible. We recommend Judas Iscariot as your controller and right-hand man.

Sincerely yours,

The report was reprinted from the UM Christian Advocate, 1992.

Jesus spent an entire night in prayer before he chose the Twelve. Three of them are recorded as having uttered only a single sentence. Six did not say anything the gospel writers thought worthy of recording. Yet, Jesus, the Son of God, chose these very ordinary men to undertake the most important enterprise in the world.

The apostles had glaring faults and weaknesses, but Jesus used them wonderfully. My personal feeling is that God chose such men to demonstrate what God can do with ordinary, powerless everyday people. Jesus wanes all who hear His voice to work within the kingdom of God. In doing this, we will find ourselves and find what we really wane from life. We cannot build our lives around a substantial center until we build it around Jesus. Jesus will cake us from where we are and lead us to where He wants us to go. And no one can stop Him!

Are you ready? God can use you. Who would have thought that relatively powerless persons could bring shifts in history? Gandhi, an unsuccessful lawyer, adopted the teachings of the Sermon on the Mount and the writings of Tolstoy and became the key to bringing independence to India, because he was ready. Rosa Parks could not have known that when she refused to obey a law that she considered evil and nonsensible, her action would spark a civil rights movement that would be felt around the world. But she was ready. When Dr. King was asked what pivotal event spurred him into action as a leader of the underclass, he pointed to Rosa Parks' boldness.

Nelson Mandela was given a life sentence in prison. Yet, he was released to bring a shift in the politics of South Africa at a critical juncture. Many thought that change would not come. However, a transition to a more just society came peacefully under his leadership after he was unexpectedly released from prison. He was ready.

Mother Teresa, a humble nun, who spent her life serving the sick, the very poor, the outcast, is being considered for sainthood for her simple acts of kindness. She was ready.Scripture reveals many women who were powerless, yet they performed powerful tasks and were given special honor by God. Let's read about some of these heroines: Miriam, sister of Moses and Aaron, was a prophetess and a songwriter (Micah 6:4). Deborah, also a prophetess, was a judge in Israel (Judges 4:4). Eve, Adam's wife, was the mother of all and I mean all living people (Genesis 3:20). Anna was a faithful witness, a prophetess of the tribe of Asher in Christ's time (Luke 2:36). There was the Samaritan woman with a sordid background, who founded the water of life at the well. The Bible tells us that when she broached the subject of the Messiah, Jesus said, "I who speak to you am He" (John 4:26). Never before nor never again that He declared Himself this plainly until the night of His betrayal. This woman was powerless and became powerful.

Lydia's hospitality was indicative of her faith. God opened her heart to believe and she opened her house, begged Paul and the other missionary to come and stay at her house. She was a convert of Thyatira (Acts 16:11-15). There were many other powerless women: Sarah, Rahab, Ruth, Hannah, Mary and Martha, Mary Magdalene. Paul named a few in his writings. Both women and men who stood up and were anointed to do the work of God became powerful after having been powerless. God is still choosing powerless people, males and females, to perform powerful tasks. Are you ready?

Jesus said, "All power is given unto me in heaven and in earth" Matt. 28:18. In verses 19 and 20 Jesus continues, "Go ye therefore, and teach all nations, baptizing them in the name of the Father, and of the Son and of the Holy Spirit, teaching them to observe all things that I have commanded you: and, lo, I am with you always, even unto the end of the age."

Jesus uses powerless people for powerful tasks. And all one needs to do is to give Him free-reign to be used. Put your all in His hands.

Let us pray: Father, help us to commit our work, our lives, and our all to you and use us as your instruments. In Jesus' name. Amen

LORD, SPARE MY FAMILY AND ALL THAT WE POSSESS

"Lord, spare my family and all that we possess." Satan is at work constantly trying to destroy communities, nations and families. My belief is that at this hour God is going to do that which needs to be done in the lives of His people, individually and collectively. If you are open to receive God's help, God is ready and willing to give help in every area of your life. From the terror that struck our great nation, and from the terror all over the world, all of us need to pray without ceasing. We see that the forces of destruction are loose. I pray that we realize that there is only one great force that Can stop this evil. That force is God Almighty. We need to adhere to 2 Chronicles 7:14 which reads, "If my people who are called by My name will humble themselves, and pray and seek My face, and turn from will forgive wicked ways, then will '11 hear from heaven, and forgive their sin and heal their land." We need to pray, "Lord, spare my family and all that we possess. That family may include not only your personal family but your Christian family or families as well.

Let us look back for a moment to the story recorded in Joshua. The old familiar scene is Israel's conquest of the city of Jericho. Israel brings great destruction to the city of Jericho; yet, in spite of the destruction, one woman was able to save herself, her family, and all of their possessions. The scene in America may be different. The characters are different, but the situation has not changed much. Sure Israel was at war when this incident occurred. We, too, are at war abroad and we are at war at home. We are at war! Our servicemen and women are fighting and dying that we may be free. Unless we get back to God, our foundation; seek His help; and take our families back to God, the turmoil will continue and escalate. I want you to know there is a solution to the turmoil in this world and that solution is Jesus Christ. When affliction presses your soul and waves of trouble roll and you need someone to help you, He is the One. I'm here to tell you that if we ever needed the Lord we need Him now!

Joshua 2:1-3 states, Now Joshua the son of Nun sent out two men from Acacia Grove to spy secretly, saying, "Go, view the land, especially Jericho.' So they went, and came to the house of a harlot named Rahab, and lodged there." The king of Jericho knew that the men had entered to search out the country and he knew that they had gone to Rahab's house. He sent to Rahab saying, "Bring out the men who have come to you, who have entered your house, for they have come to search out our country." Rahab took the two men and hid them. She replied, "Yes, the men came to me, but I did not know where they were from." Now you see these men, these spies: came incognito. They thought that they were perfectly disguised and that no one knew who they were. They wanted to get a good view of the city and to find out what was going on within the city' You know the story, but I am going to tell it anyway. The strangers went to Rahab's house. When they got in, the word got out that there were some strangers in town who look like the children of Israel; and they were last seen in the vicinity of Rahab's house. There is always someone watching in the vicinity. Rahab knew who they were. When the time came to shut down the city gate, she told her countrymen that the spies had gone out, to pursue them and overtake them. Taking her directions, the men left and the gate was closed. Before the spies retired, she went up to them and said, "I know that the Lord has given you the land and that your terror has fallen upon us. Not only do I know this but this whole town is panic stricken." She knew that God was with the men.

The people of Jericho had heard how the waters of the Red Sea had dried up within the Red Sea and what the Israelites did to the Kings of the Amorites who were on the other side. Sihon and Og were destroyed. Chapter 21 of Joshua tells of the destruction of Sihon. Israelites were trying to pass through after leaving Egypt on their way to the Promised Land.

All they wanted to do was to take a short cut through the land of the Amorites and Sihon. Not being permitted to do so, Sihon and the King of Basham were destroyed. These events went down in history as part of God's awesome power to destroy those who try to hinder the march of His church and His holy people. The Psalmist in Psalm 136 talks about giving thanks unto the God of gods! For His mercy endures forever. He tells how God slew famous Kings, and he named Og and Basham. It is bad b to tangle with God and get defeated. God will hang your name in history, and centuries later people will read how the Lord caused you to lay wasted because you tried to stop Him.

Rahab, the harlot, said to the spies, "Your reputation preceded you. I know who you are! "Now therefore, I beg you, swear to me by the Lord, since I have shown you kindness, that you also will show kindness to my father's house and give me a true token, and spare my father, my mother, my brothers, my sisters, and all that they have, and deliver our lives from death." So the men answered her. Our lives for yours, if none of you tell this business of ours. And it shall be when the Lord has given us the land, that we deal kindly and truly with you" (Joshua 2: 12-14). She simply said, "We know you are coming, we know what's going to happen, but I just want to know, will you save me and my family and all we possess?"

Today, we live in a panic-stricken nation; panic is present in our cities, states, and all over the world. The criminals are free in the streets, and we are locked up in our own homes. Some folks are locked in while they are on the inside to protect themselves from those with whom they live. Upon whom are we depending? Is God our Lord? I hope so. The world is being destroyed. The devil's army has been released, but I just want you to know, in spite of all that is happening I am calling out to God, "Lord, save me and my family and all we possess." You can do the same. I personally do not believe that any one man, nor the United Nations, nor a Peace Treaty can save the nations of the world. How can a Peace Treaty save the world when all of the heads of the nations sit down and there in no chair reserved for the Prince of Peace?

If there is any salvation, we must find a way to make a peace pact with God. Rahab, a heathen and a prostitute, was saved because she demonstrated faith. Rahab was willing to risk everything she had for a

God she barely knew. This tells us that we must not judge a person by his or her background, lifestyle, or appearance. We must be very careful and more Christ like. This tells me that we must be willing to risk everything for the One and Only God, as well.

I am told that Rahab's house was built so that she could look over the inner wall into the city; then she could see the outside from the outer wall. So she took these spies and using a scarlet cord (red in color, which is a symbol of the blood of Jesus) to let them down the window that overlooked the outer wall. In answer to her request the spies said, "Yes, but when we return we will not recognize your house from anyone else's house unless you display this same scarlet cord. And when we see the window where the scarlet cord is hanging, we are going to make sure that anyone that is in this house is spared." Don't you see the same thing happened in Egypt on the night of The Passover. The spies said, "Get them under the Blood." That's all I am trying to tell you. We must get under the blood of Jesus. If you are wondering how you can change various situations in your home, in your families, in your communities, in our nation, tell them about the blood of Jesus. Put your love ones under the blood of Jesus. If you want your families, love ones and associates saved, you have got to get them under the "blood of Jesus."

I am told that Rahab sent the spies to the mountain and told them to hide there for three days until the pursuers had returned. "Afterward you may go your way" she said.

Joshua said, "Where are the spies that came into the city? You fellows know Rahab, go in and get her. Get everything that is under that red string and bring them out here. And when you get them in safety, then send in the men with swords and kill everything left. But don't kill anything until you get Rahab, her family and all of their possessions out here." Rahab and her family got all their possessions and were saved.

Read Joshua Chapter 6, verses 22-25, and you will see that Rahab, her family and all she possesses were saved.

The devil is saying that you think you have seen something in these cities, in the world, but you haven't seen anything yet. He said that he is going to keep on killing until he has killed all. But God said, "Wait a minute, devil, you are not going to do anything to my children under the 'blood of Jesus.'" God is telling us, His believers, to pray and get our families, friends, and associates on safe ground under the "Blood of Jesus." He who is in us is greater than he who is in the world. We must have faith in God. Rahab had faith household were that she would be saved, and she and her house saved, God is an awesome God, holding, all power in His hand. Have faith in God!

Jesus told us to have faith in God. Some of you are wondering, Why is there so much turmoil?" I will tell you why. You have prayed. but even while you prayed, you did not believe. You had no faith. Some of you may believe me today, tonight. Let me warn you that things will not change until you exercise your faith. Don't you realize that it is impossible to please God without faith? God is telling you to exercise your faith. If He saved a harlot, He will save you. If you believe that you need stronger faith, ask God to increase your faith. Personally, I believe that God has given us enough faith to last forever. We just have to use it.

Do you really believe that you can hold on to God and that God can change circumstances for you? If you believe this, confess it with your mouth say, "God is not going to let the devil do another thing to me or my family. We are on safe ground, Holy ground." WE ARE UNDER THE BLOOD OF JESUS. JESUS' BLOOD WILL NEVER LOOSE ITS POWER. THERE IS LIFE IN THE BLOOD. Now Praise Him! Praise Him! Praise Him! God lives in the praises of His people. Thank Him! I challenge you to cover yourself, your family, and others with the Blood of Jesus. Lord, spare my family and all we possess, in Jesus' name. Amen

THE LORD IS ON MY SIDE;
I WILL NOT FEAR

SCRIPTURE: Psalm 118:5--6a

I read a story about a humble woman walking along a road carrying a large bundle of clothes on her head. It was noon and the heat was suffocating, but still she walked. A man driving by saw her and, sympathizing, he stopped and offered her a ride. The woman got in the car and made herself comfortable in the rear seat. After driving awhile, the man saw that the woman still carried the bundle of clothes on her head. Ma'am, he said, "Put your bundle of clothes on the seat. You need not carry it. The car will carry you and your bundle, too!"

Isn't that what we do with the "bundles" within our lives? We carry them on our own when help is available. All we have to do is deliver our concerns to our Lord, who promises to help us all the days of our lives. The Psalmist in writing Psalm 118 knew that, for ne he said, "I called upon the Lord in my distress: The Lord answered fear" and set me in a broad place. The Lord is on my side; I will not fear" (Psalm 118:5-6a).

Psalm 118 is ordinarily categorized as a song of thanksgiving, Like other Psalms of this type, it recounts and celebrates experiences \ of deliverances. However, Psalm 118 is unique. While the speaker for most of the Psalm is an individual "I," the distress recounted seems to suggest a crisis of national proportions. Some scholars concluded the "I" is the king of Israel speaking to the people, but this is elusive.

Verse five offers a succinct definition of the deliverance. The Hebrew root of the noun distress has the sense of "restricted," "narrow," "tight."

Out of my distress, I called upon the Lord.... All nations surrounded me..., they surrounded me like bees. Have you ever seen bees surround a person? I have. My son was four years old. We lived on the beautiful island of Guam. In our yard, there were red and pink sweet hibiscus. He and his friend were playing and he fell among the flowers, I heard him cry out, "Mommy, Mommy." I ran to him and saw that he was covered from head to toe with bees. I called upon the Lord and He heard my call. I fought the bees and the child was safe. Yes, I took him to the medical center for treatment, but they found only one small knot under his arm. I can identify with the Psalmist as he called upon the Lord. The Psalmist continued, "I was pushed hard, so that I was falling." Reading further, one could say that he even might have been ill. Verses 17 and 18 give credence to this statement. We don't know his total struggle. We do know that the Lord heard his cry, answered him and set him free. Therefore, he could proclaim, "The Lord is on my side; I will not fear" (Psalm 118:6). Will is a strong word. He was saying, "Fear is against my will."

Our world is filled with fear. Some people are afraid to stay home alone during stormy weather. Others have burglar bars and burglar alarms. Some are afraid to leave their homes. Some are afraid of their neighbors, family members...children are afraid of, parents and parents are afraid of children. Does any of this remind you of Bible Prophecies? I heard a young black man on the evening news say that he was questioned by the police for driving a new car in a certain neighborhood. I believe that many activities of this kind are common in today's society. He said that he was afraid not knowing what the policeman would do. We live in a world of fear. Children are now afraid of the fire alarm in school, teachers are afraid of some of their students, and parents are afraid of their children attending school. People are afraid of and on their jobs. There is the fear of terrorism, the fear of flying, of driving, of people. There are fears of and in relationships. Do you realize that fear is a satanic force that works against society at every opportunity? The good news is that faith is a creative force that God uses to build and uplift His people. The devil challenges the promises of God with fear-filled lies of his own.

As children of God, we will not fear! Why? God has not given us the spirit of fear, but of power and love, and a sound mind (2 Tim.1:7). We will not fear because God is on our side. We will not fear because fear is activated by the devil. We will not fear because faith is God's source of power, and we operate in faith. We will not fear because fear is destructive. Fear is a killer. Fear is not an ingredient in God's success plan. We will not fear because fear wipes out God's plan. Why fear things that we think are going to happen, have happened or will never happen? We will not fear, for the Lord is on our side. We will not fear! Faith produces life. Faith takes a curse and turns it into a blessing. Faith takes non-caring and turns it into resurrection. If God is on our side, whom shall we fear?

God spoke through Isaiah 43:1-2 telling us, "Fear not, I have redeemed thee. I have called thee by name; thou are mine. When thou passest through the water, I will be with thee." God is telling His People over and over not to fear. There is no fear in love. Perfect love casteth out fear because fear hath torment. He that feareth is not made perfect in love (1 John 4:18). Fear must be replaced with faith, trust, belief, hope, and steadfastness that produce faithfulness. Why? The Lord is on our side. Fear and faith are opposites. Without faith it is impossible to serve God (Heb.11: 6).

Faith is the New Testament word for the Old Testament Trust, which appears in the Old Testament 105 times. The prophets deepen the meaning of faith in several ways. For Isaiah (7:1.9), security does not rest in political power but in trust in God; in fact, the totality of life must be based on trust in God. Isaiah 7-9 says, if you will not believe, surely you shall not be established. Proverbs 3:5 tell us to Trust in the Lord with all thine heart. Saints, we must totally trust in God. The Bible tells us, "But without faith it is impossible to please Him (Hebrews 6a).

Jesus told His disciples to "Have faith in God" (Mark 11:22). Romans 10:17 tells us that faith (*pistis*) cometh by hearing and hearing by the Word (*rhema*). I want to tell you that faith is not a trophy to put on display as an exhibit; it is not a broach or pin for impressing people. Faith is a gift from God. Faith is knowing that God can't lie. It is the confident assurance that something we want is going to happen. Jesus used the tiny mustard seed to describe faith. "If you have faith as a mustard seed, you will say to this mountain, 'Move from here to there,' and it will move; and nothing will be impossible for you" (Matthew 17:20). At times I feel that my faith is as small as a mustard seed... Sometimes, I feel that I am all alone here and

God od has to speak to me and say, "I am with you always, trust me." He had to remind me of who I am and of whose I am. With faith, one will be able to withstand any challenge.

Children of God, faith knows that God will do what God said He would do. Permit me to name a few of the Old Testament saints who had faith:

It was faith that Abel obeyed God and brought an offering that pleased God.

It was by faith that Abraham trusted God, and when God

told him to leave home, he obeyed.

It was by faith that Sarah became a mother in her old age.

It was by faith Enoch was taken away so that he did not see death and was not found because God had taken him.

It was by faith that Rahab, the harlot, did not die with all the others because she believed in God and His power.

It was by faith that the Samaritan woman found the water of life at the well for she said, "Come, see a man who told me all things that I ever did. Could this be the Christ?" (John 4:29)

It was faith that the men of the city of Sychar went back to the well where they all met Jesus.

It was by faith that many of the Samaritans of that city believed in Him because of the word of the woman who testified.

It was by faith that Lydia opened her house to Paul and the missionaries and begged them to come. Lydia had the honor of hosting in her living room the earliest meeting of the first church ever established in Europe.

There were those in the New Testament that were healed by faith. By faith, many miracles occurred.

Throughout the centuries, faith still worked its miracles.

By faith, Thomas Jefferson founded the University of Virginia when he was 76.

By faith, Dr. Mary McLeod Bethune started a school, Bethune-Cookman, with one dollar and fifty cents.

By faith, Dr. Martin Luther King, Jr. changed the course of our nation.

By faith, many great men and women of various ethnic groups (African-Americans, Asians, Caucasians, Jews, Hispanics, Native American, and all other groups) have made great contributions to our nation and our world.

Peter Bohler's words to the great Methodist Leader, John Wesley, were as follows: "To preach faith till you have it and because you have it, you will preach faith." We are in a war, and God needs bold soldiers in His army, soldiers who are nor afraid to preach faith. We must preach faith!

Dr. E. Stanley Jones penned the following affirmation in his book, Transformed by Thorns: "I am inwardly fashioned for faith, not fear. Fear is not my native land; faith is. I am so made that worry and anxiety are sands in the machinery of life; faith is the oil. I live better by faith and confidence than by fear, doubt and anxiety. In anxiety and worry, my being is gasping for breath-these are not my native air. But in faith and confidence, I breathe freely-these are my native air. A [Johns Hopkins] 'University doctor says 'We do not know why it is that worriers die sooner than the non-worriers, but that is a fact. But I, who am simple of mind, think I know; we are inwardly constructed in nerve and tissue, brain cell and soul, for faith and not for fear. God made us that way. To live by worry is to live against reality (p 95).

I believe Mickey Rivers, a one time outfielder for the Texas Rangers professional basketball team, captured this philosophy of life when he said, "Ain't no sense worrying about things you got control over, because if you got control over them, ain't no sense worrying. And there ain't no sense worrying about things you got no control over either, because if you got no control over them, ain't no sense worrying."

Let me give a part of my personal testimony. By faith, I was healed from arthritis in my shoulder, back, neck and arm. It was by faith that when I was really ill in the hospital and the doctors couldn't and out what was wrong, Dr. Jesus stepped in and by His being there I was healed. The Lord is on my side. By faith) I was not bruised when a drunk driver hit my car while fleeing from a policeman and driving at a speed between 85 and 95 miles an hour• My car never moved. The Lord is on my side. By faith, God put out, a Ere that was in my kitchen with a gush of wind, and the Chief of the Fire Department couldn't understand. The Lord is on my side. By faith, an Angel stopped and changed a flat tire for me. After thanking him and getting in my car, I had a strange feeling to fall upon me; I couldn't help looking back to see where the man went. There was no man visible. That's why I know that the man was an angel The Lord is on my side. I have seen miracle after miracle because God is on my side.

In concluding this sermon, I want you to know that I am not ashamed to testify about the goodness of God. The Lord is on my side: I will not fear. With Holy Spirit Power, I have stepped over the line. I have made my decision. I am a servant, an ambassador for the Lord. The Lord is on my side; I will not fear. My past is redeemed, my present makes sense, and my future is secured. The Lord is on my side; I will not fear.

I don't need preeminence, prosperity, position, promotion or popularity. I have the Lord on my side; I will not fear. I don't have to be first, right, tops, recognized, praised, regarded nor rewarded. The Lord is on my side; I will not fear. I now am living by faith, leaning on God's presence, walking by patience, lifting Jesus up and blessing others through prayer and labor. The Lord is on my side; I will not fear. I challenge you to make sure that the Lord is on your side and you will not fear.

THE FINAL JUDGMENT OF NATIONS/GENTILE NATIONS

SUBTITLE: ARE YOU A SHEEP OR A GOAT?

SCRIPTURE: MATTTHEW 25:31-46

A long-time friend, whom a minister met in a distant city, once asked the minister, "How many members do you have in your church?"

"One thousand," the preacher replied.

"Really!" "And how many of them are active."

"All of them." "About two hundred are active for the Lord; all of the others are active for the devil."

Are you active for the Lord or the devil? Are you a sheep or a goat? The sheep are active for the Lord, and the goats are active for the devil. The sheep as described in Matthew 25 did not know, that it was Jesus who was thirsty, hungry, or in prison. This minds me of an occurrence that took place under my watch at a barbeque stand. One lonely night, I stood by the window wishing that someone would come and purchase a sandwich or a soft drink. At 10:30 p.m., the stand would close. At approximately 10:15 p.m., a stranger walked to the window and asked for directions to the Salvation Army. He was given the directions and sent on his way. Immediately, there was this great impulse to call him back and feed him. He was called just before he disappeared into the deep darkness. When asked whether he was hungry and wanted a sandwich, he replied, "Yes." I gave him food and a drink. He thanked me, blessed me and departed.

After his departure, there was a strange feeling and without voicing it, I knew that he was an angel.

What is the purpose of the sheep and goat parable? The purpose of the parable is to inform us that Jesus, "King of Kings," in His glory will come and all the holy angels will come with Him. And then He will sit on His throne of His glory to judge all nations. At this judgment, He will separate the sheep from the goats. The disciples understood this picturesque language because the shepherds in the land of Palestine separated their flock every evening as they returned to the sheep cote (Ezekiel 34:17). We are told that at twilight the shepherds stood at the gate to the sheepfold and tapped their rods on the ground. The sheep went to the right, and the goats went to the left. Who are the sheep and who are the goats that Jesus is identifying within this parable?

The sheep are the saved. They are those who visited the sick, fed the hungry, clothe the naked, and gave drink to the thirsty. They have responded to Jesus as He had shown Himself as one of the least ones in need of help. They are the ones that will sit on His right hand side in a place of honor, authority and power. They did not deny Jesus. In His address to those designated as His sheep' Jesus bestowed blessings and benefits. During the tribulation period, they will minister to the Jewish remnant, the brethren (the elect of Israel). Through ministering to the remnant, the Gentile Christians proclaimed their faith In Jesus Christ. Jesus said, "He who receives you receives Me, and he who receives Me receives Him who sent Me. . . And whoever gives one of these little ones only a cup of cold water in the name of a disciple, assuredly, I say to you, he shall by no means lose his reward" (Matthew 10:40-42).

Yes, during the tribulation period the Gentile will show mercy and love the persecuted Jews. Their good deed classifies them as sheep. We realize that salvation is by grace alone, but the writer of Hebrews reminds us that Christ will not forget our work of labor of love which we have done in His name (Hebrews 6:10).

The goats are the unsaved. They are those who never visit the sick, nor feed the hungry, nor clothe the naked, nor give water to the thirsty. They are those who put all of their belongings in the barns (banks) for themselves and their own, and they never reach out to help others. They are those who rob others and think nothing of it. They are those who do all manner of evil against others. They are those who lie, steal, cheat and some kill. They are those who Jesus put on His left side. They are the workers of iniquity. They are the doomed. The goats departed from God and as a result, Christ tells them to depart from Him. Where are the goats sent? It is not a place of It is not a place of comfort. It is not a place that you want to be. It is a place of weeping and gnashing of teeth. It is a place of darkness. It is a place of no return. It is a place of hell. It is a place that I do not want any part of. What about you?

John Townsend in his writing of The Sheep and Goats said, "The behavior of the goats is diametrically opposite of the behavior of the sheep. Instead of serving others during the day of God's wrath, they turned inward and looked out for number one, themselves. They are cursed because of their omission. The sentence is passed, the verdict is swift, and the doom is fixed." (Excerpts from Townsend's message, p. 17).

Don't you see it?
The sheep hear Him say "Come."
The goats heard Him say "Go."
The sheep will live, and their lives will be eternal, never ending.
The goats shall go away into everlasting punishment.
The judgment is for eternity.

The King expects us as Christians to do His will. We have major precedents in the Bible to warrant a commission to minister to the needy of this world. We see this from the denunciation of Israel by Old Testament Prophets for displaying covenant unfaithfulness in its lack of care for the poor, all the way to the Book of James. Christ has identified Himself with the poor, the destitute, the oppressed, the naked, the marginalized. He identifies with those who are living in the margins, the least who are looking for a better life. Christ clearly said that when we minister "to the least," we are ministering unto Him, personally. Matthew 8:17 tells us that He identified as one with His people. People, when we neglect to minister unto the least, we are rejecting Christ. The goats failed to minister. The goats lived selfishly. They were comfortable and spiritually blind. They refused to see God's glorious love for all mankind. Jesus is coming back to judge! Many Scriptures tell us that God's judgment will be administered by Jesus, the Christ. To name a few of the Scriptures, read John 5:22, 27; Acts 10:41; Romans 14:10 and many others.

This judgment is not of the Great White Throne found in Revelation 20:11-15. At this judgment, Christ, "the King," will judge the nations in His earthly kingdom. At the Great White Throne, the kingdom is no longer in view. Right, the earth has vanished. I am told that at this judgment, there will be no books opened. At the Great White Throne, there will be books opened (Revelation 20:12).

Within this parable, Jesus has provided insight into His second coming. There will be those saying, "Lord, when did we see you hungry, or thirsty, or sick, or in jail?" And He will say what? "In as much as you did it unto one of the least of these my brethren, you did it unto me" (Matthew 25:44-45).

Now there is another group, the unsaved, called goats. I believe that there is a hell and a heaven because it is in the Word. Hell is an Eternal Place according to Matthew 21 verse 41. God prepared it for satan and his angels. They have no choice, but you have a choice to enter into satan's prepared hell or the believer's prepared heaven (John 14:1-6). Christ the judge will say to the living wicked, those on the left hand side, the goats, at the judgment, "Depart from me; you are cursed, into the everlasting fire prepared for the devil and his angels" (Matthew 25:46). Is this what you want Christ to say to you? If these are not the words that you want to hear, then turn your life around. He will give you a new heart and put a new spirit within you. He will take the heart of stone out of your flesh and give you a heart of flesh (Ezekiel 36:26).

The evil ones satan, the antichrist, and the false prophets will be cast in hell, where they will be tormented day and night forever and ever (Rev. 20:10). At the last judgment, all of the wicked dead will be resurrected and will stand in body, soul and spirit before God at the Great White Throne. Christ will be the judge (John 5:22). When the wicked see His resurrected, glorified human body, they will know that He has every right to judge them and cast them into the lake of fire along with their gods, the evil triad.

HELL IS NOT FOR ME! WHAT ABOUT YOU? IT WAS NOT MADE FOR YOU, AND ONLY YOU HAVE THE CHOICE TO GO OR NOT TO GO THERE. GOATS WILL NOT ACCEPT THIS CHALLENGE TO STAY OUT HELL BUT SHEEP WILL! ARE YOU A GOAT OR SHEEP?

REPENT AMERICA and PRAY

SCRIPTURE: 11 Chronicles 7:14; 1
Thessalonians 5:17,22 John 14: 27; Isaiah 48:22

Americans will never again be complacent about security in any form. Evil humans attacked our homeland, and our view of the world will never be the same. We watched helplessly as the terrorists hit the Twin Towers of the World Trade Center and the Pentagon and many asked, "How could this happen?" Some of us couldn't say a thing, while others cried out to God. We prayed with love for those who never found their loved ones, for all those who had love ones on the planes, and for the heroes and heroines who were involved. That is all we could do at that moment, to pray, and we must continue pray. Our President, declared war against terrorism, a war that he says we shall win. We realize that the terrorist attack was the most egregious assault on the continental United States, ever. Where do we go from here? What must we the populace of this great country do?

We have been told that the Sunday after the destruction the World Trade Center and the striking of the Pentagon, most of the churches across the nation were filled with humble persons. Are these people continuously attending church? Has the nation reverted back in the old materialist, non-caring attitude? I believe we have. I also believe that we are within a crucial period within our nation, due not only to the effects of the war, but also to the many social and inhumane ills that rear their heads. I know that the most effective weapon we have is prayer, not fear. Now is the time for revival in our churches, on our streets, in our storefronts, even on our football fields. Americans everywhere should be praying. The little children should be praying. One has only to listen to the broadcast media or read the newspapers to know that we are living in dangerous times. However, we should not fear. God spoke to Solomon after he dedicated the Temple, and He is speaking to America today. He is telling us to dedicate our lives to Him. In Second Chronicles 7:14, God tells us, "If My people who are called by My name will humble themselves, and pray and seek my face, and turn from their wicked ways, then I will hear from heaven, and will forgive their sin and heal their land." It is time for praying, seeking, repenting and humbling ourselves before the King of Kings. God continues by saying, "Now My eyes will be open and My ears attentive to prayer made in this place" v. 15. God is the same God. Shouldn't we recognize this as King Solomon did? The King prayed, "Lord God of Israel, there is no God in heaven or earth like you, who keep Your covenant and mercy with Y°1.5 servants who walk before You with all their hearts" (2 chronicles 6:14).

Second Timothy 3:1--9 warns us that in the last days perilous times shall come. Zola Levitt has warned us for many years: an Islamic-extremist assault against democracy/Christianity. He contends that United States was considered by some to be in more danger than Israel, and that Israel is only a pretext for what may become an assault on the whole world of free nations.

Zola in his letter of October 2001 wrote, "I certainly hope our government realizes the gravity of this assault. If the Lord tarries and we make no adequate response, there is a chance that the Militants will plunge the world into a new Dark Age." It is prayer and repentance time, America. The Prophet Jonah was told to take a message of judgment to Nineveh. When Jonah told Nineveh to repent and turn from its wicked ways, the people of Nineveh obeyed. As a result of this obedience, God spared that great city for approximately 85 years. This tells us that God's first will is not judgment, but revival. I believe that God will revive America if America will repent and pray. We must pray without ceasing. Never again will we feel that we are over here and the enemies are over there. We have let the enemies within our territory; thus, we were caught unprepared. Doesn't that make you think? Will you be unprepared when Jesus comes back to gather His own? Are you letting satan creep into your lives? Do you realize that satan will use your own devices against you Pray that satan will flee from you and yours. Isaiah 48:22 tells us that God says there is no peace for the wicked. Let us work for the Lord in times like these. We need to pray for our churches, the Congress and all who are in authority, everyday. It matters not whether he or she is Democrat, Republican or Independent; all will bow to God.

> 1 Timothy 2:1-4 says, "Therefore I exhort first all that supplications, prayer, intercession, and giving of thanks be made for all men, for kings and all who are in authority, that we may lead a quiet and peaceable life in all godliness and reverence. For this is good and acceptable in the and t sight of God Our Savior; who desires all men to be saved o come to the knowledge of the truth."

Pray and don't faint. Christ urges us not to cease praying when we do not see our problems disappear immediately. "Then He spoke a parable to them, that men always ought to pray and not to lose heart" (Luke 18:1). Repent and pray America and give God thanks!

True, we face a world of crisis and uncertainty, but we as Christians have the assurance that God is with us. Jesus said, "Peace I leave you, My peace I give to you: not as the world gives do I give to you. Let not your heart be troubled, neither let it be afraid" (John 14:27). Fear has gripped the nation, but we can't serve God and serve the evil one, too. We must believe God and pray for this great nation. We know God will hear and answer our Prayers. 1 John 5:15 says, "And if we know that He hears us, whatever we ask, we know that we have the petition that we have asked of Him." AMERICA REPENT and PRAY for the Healing of our Nation and the Nations of the World.

Fred Kaan captured the equation "For the Healing of the Nations" in his hymn when he wrote:

> For the healing of the nation, Lord we pray
> with one accord; for a just equal sharing of
> the things that earth affords; to a life of love
> in action helps us rise and pledge our word.
> Lead us forward into freedom; from despair

your world release, that redeemed from war and hatred
All may come and go in peace. Show us how through
care and goodness fear will die and hope increase (hope
increase) fear will die and hope increase.

You, Creator God, have written your great name on
Human-kind; for our growing in your likeness bring
The life of Christ to mind, that by our response and service
Earth its destiny may find, earth its destiny may find.

(United Methodist Hymnal, p.428. Published by Hope Publishing Co.,
Published in the Methodist Hymnal Book of the U M Worship; Nashville,
Tenn. 1989)

A friend of mine, Dr. Paul Shimek, Jr. provided me with his Sermon titled "Jerusalem: Countdown to Crises." With his permission, I have selected excerpts from his sermon "Jerusalem: Countdown to Crises to include in my book. All must read this, for God is still and will always be in control of the world. Also included is Dr. Shimek's Autobiography.

Dr. Paul Shimek's Autobiography Being instructed by the certification division of the Escambia County School Board administration to place a resume on file for public inspection, the following is submitted. I was born on a farm in Arkansas on October 7, 1931, and for seventeen years of my life worked with my family raising rice, oats and wheat. I joined the U.S. Navy when I became 17 and served as an enlisted person for two years before I entered the U. S. Naval Academy. My first exposure to Russian was there at Annapolis. Upon graduation, I was assigned to the training command in Pensacola and went through flight training here and subsequently in Texas for jet fighter training. I served in the Western Pacific on three aircraft carriers in a fighter squadron. I resigned my commission after 13 years in the U. S. Navy and entered law school at the University of Florida, Gainesville in 1961 and commenced practice of law in 1964 and practiced for 26 years.

Then I commenced my teaching career at Jubilee Christian Academy, Pensacola, where I taught high school math, Russian and Bible. I also taught

Russian language at Pensacola Junior College for four years. In 2000, I had an opportunity to go to University of South Alabama to study four years to obtain a BA Russian language. I was dual enrolled at the University of West Florida where I received in April 2005 a master's degree in secondary education. I am certified to teach Russian and math in Florida high schools.

The opportunity to gain more education was a Veterans. Administration benefit awarded me by virtue of a disability caused by a severe knee injury that occurred while on active duty during the Korean Conflict.

I have a history minor also from the University of South Alabama. I am married, and we have two sons who are also attorneys practicing in Pensacola and Atlanta.

My specialty is Russian language, but I also love teaching math and history. I was a varsity wrestler at the U.S. Naval Academy and today am an avid swimmer in perfect health.

Respectfully submitted,
Paul Shimek, Jr.

JERUSALEM, COUNTDOWN O CRISES

SCRIPTURE: Matthew 23:27

Let us talk about Jerusalem and the effort our country is making to implement what is called the "Roadmap to Peace." The "Roadmap to Peace" is forcing Israel to divide up the land that God gave to the Jewish people. God's response is that He is going to bring judgment upon the nations that participate in this process of dividing. If we continue to force Israel to give up land to the enemies 0. t Israel, then the judgment of God will come to the United States In unprecedented proportions. There is a connection between the situation of 9,000 (nine thousand) Jews being evicted from their homes forcibly in Gaza, and now living in tents, and the thousands of Americans who were expelled from their homes caused by the answer If you have a better tremendous work of nature we call Katrina. If you have a better answer upon any research authority including the Bible, I would like to hear it.

We will discuss Jerusalem in Bible history because Jerusalem is the city of God. All other cities are known by their architecture, or by their wealth, or by their size. But not Jerusalem — it is known as God's city. Next, we want to discuss Jesus and Jerusalem. What did Jesus see in the future as He went on the Mount of Olives over the city of Jerusalem? Next we want to discuss Jerusalem and Iran, since that country is now developing a nuclear weapon. We know they are working on it and diplomacy is having no retarding beneficial effect. Finally, we want to discuss Jerusalem and the Antichrist and the seven (7) signs telling when Jesus is returning.

Matt.23:37-39: "Oh Jerusalem, Jerusalem, the one who kills the prophets and stones those who are sent to her! How often I wanted to gather your children together, as a hen gathers her chicks under her wings, but you were not willing! See! Your house is left to you desolate; for I say to you, you shall see Me no more till you say, Blessed is He who comes in the name of the LORD!"

Matt. 24:3: "Now as He sat on the Mount of Olives, the disciples came to Him privately, saying, "Tell us, when will these things be? And what will be the sign of your coming, and of the end of the age?"

First, let's consider Jerusalem in Bible history. Psalm 132:13 says, "The Lord has chosen Zion. He has desired it for His habitation." 2 Chronicles 6:6: "I, God, have chosen Jerusalem that My name might be there." Psalm 137:5, David is speaking: If I forget you oh Jerusalem, let my right hand forget its cunning; let my tongue cleave to the roof of my mouth." The essence of that verse is as follows : David is a musician, who if he loses his ability to play and loses his ability to sing, means that to him life will have lost its significance. He is saying, "If I forget Jerusalem, then there is no reason to have life." Jerusalem is first mentioned in the Bible in Genesis 14:18 when Melchizedek, King of Salem, met Abraham and blessed him. (almost 4,000 years ago). Keep in mind that every mention of Jerusalem in the Scripture has a message from God to those who love Him. This isn't a walk through history, but a walk through the blessings of God for you. The blessings Melchizedek gave Abraham are recorded in the Scripture: "And blessed be God most high who has delivered your enemies into your hands." God's message for you and for me today is that God has your enemies physically and spiritually in His control, and He has already defeated them. God will deliver your enemies into your hands! The battle has already been won. The enemy that is attacking your marriage, your business, your children, or your financial future — God has already defeated that enemy! The enemy who is attacking your mind, your health, your peace of mind, and bringing the fear, resentment and worry that follows; the enemy who is attacking your confidence for the future, that enemy God has already conquered and wrapped in chains. You have the victory because the One who goes before you is El Shaddai — the Almighty God of Israel. Praise Him!

Jerusalem is next mention in Scripture when Abraham tells his son Isaac that they are going to Mount Moriah for the giving of sacrifice. Jerusalem is not mentioned by name, but listen to the story recited in the Bible so that there is no doubt about this being Jerusalem. God told Abraham to go to Mount Moriah and sacrifice Isaac to prove his love for God. This is probably the most brutal story in all Scripture. As a father, to be asked to plunge a dagger into the heart of your son would be overwhelmingly repulsive. But without hesitation, Abraham, the father of our faith, took Isaac to the crest of Mount Moriah. Abraham possessed the dagger and the implements for the sacrifice. As they climbed the mountain, Isaac, who is only twenty-five years old, said to his one-hundred-year-old father, "Where is the lamb?" (Genesis 22:7b). Abraham, without even a blinking of the eye, looked at his son and said, "God will provide a lamb." It was cold icy faith in operation. Abraham ascended to the top of the mountain and there he bound his son, both hands and feet, and placed him on the altar. He lifted his razor sharp dagger into the air and was prepared to snuff out the life of Isaac. At the very last second an angel stopped and stayed the hand of Abraham. Right there - on the hill - an exchange Was made. A ram caught in the thicket was exchanged for the son of Abraham. Four thousand years later, on the same hill, Jesus Christ of Nazareth, the Lamb of God slain from the foundations of the earth, was bound hand and foot on a Roman cross. He suffered, bled, and died for you, me and every other person on earth. Calvary is the place of the great exchange! He took our sin and gave us forgiveness; our sickness and gave us divine healing; and our debt and gave us everlasting life; our poverty and gave us the riches of Abraham, remember, we were Gentiles outside of the covenants of Israel, and as Paul said, "Without hope and without God." Further, that God grafted us into the olive tree and made us heirs and joint heirs with Jesus Christ." He took our shame — because they crucified Him naked. He gave us a divine confidence that hell cannot shake. Nothing is impossible to those that believe. Greater is He within you than he who is within the world. So I can do all things through Jesus Christ who strengthens me. We are kings and priests unto God. Live like it, talk like it, act and think like it — you are sons and daughters of the living God!

Jerusalem appears next in the Scripture as David captures Jerusalem from the Jebusites. Do not conclude that David captured or brought into existence the city of Jerusalem. It had existed already for thousands of years, but it was totally in the hands and, possession of pagans. King David made Jerusalem the eternal and undivided capitol of Israel three thousand years ago when he captured it. This is why God loved David. David had the courage to fight the and giant had the courage to liberate Jerusalem and we will discuss why in a few moments. Jerusalem is not up for negotiation with anyone for any reason, and people in Washington, D.C. do not seem to understand that. The "Roadmap for Peace" calls for the division of Jerusalem. There are still people in the United States who believe the Bible and that belief should take precedence over decisions made in Washington, D.C. It has been suggested that Jerusalem ought to be called Jerusalem D.C., meaning David's capital. It is a biblical fact that David is going to rule there someday. The book of Ezekiel says that you are going to see him ruling there. I don't understand why we do not move our embassy from Tel Aviv to Jerusalem. After all, we have an American embassy in the capital of every nation except Israel, our only friend in the Middle East. But the State Department doesn't want to move our embassy from Tel Aviv to the capital Jerusalem because it perceives that being in Israel would tarnish our image in the region. The region already calls us the great satan, and if you have a sorry reputation, then you have no image to lose. You have already lost it, so why not recognize the capital city for what it is Washington should recognize that Jerusalem has existed for three thousand years. What was the message to the Jebusites as David captured the city? The story of David's conquest is told in 1Samuel 5, but there is a perplexing situation described in verse 8 that has recently been resolved by proper translation. That strange verse 8 has been a mystery for years, but finally we have an authenticated translation. It says, "The blind and the lame, who are hated by David's soul...." Why would David's soul hate the blind and the lame? Verse eight continues, "The blind and the lame shall not come into the house." Archaeologists recently discovered the meaning written in ancient tablets. The Jebusites, when they were attacked, would place the blind and the lame around the outer edge of the city because anyone fighting the Jebusites had to come up the mountain and through the blind and the lame. Jebusites placed a witchcraft curse upon any of their attackers. In effect, the curse stated, "Anyone of you who approaches us to fight - may you become blind and lame like these people if you attack us." David, of course, recognized that curse as the spirit of witchcraft. Therefore, he went up that water shaft and attacked the Jebusites. He defeated them, and Jerusalem became the eternal capital of Israel from that day to today. The message here is that witchcraft in any form is an illegal authority that tries to control your life. Therefore, you must recognize it and resist it. You might say that "I've never seen that and recognized it as such." Sir or Madam — if you are watching television and observed those thugs in New Orleans riding those boats and shooting and pillaging during the Katrina hurricane crises, you have seen illegal authority. Those are people who were driven by the power of the devil himself. As you know, the federal authorities finally came in and shut those people down. In the Bible, witchcraft is manifested by domination, intimidation and manipulation. Example: a husband intimidating his wife with bursts of anger tantrums; a wife controlling her husband with sex — because neither spouse's body belongs except to the other and they are equal in that regard; or finally — a mother trying to control her forty- year old daughter or son via an instantaneous illness if the children do not do what she wants them to do. Some of you have an umbilical cord three thousand miles long to the city where your child resides. Cut it off and let them go. Let them grow and make their own decisions. They should be free, for whom the Son sets free, that person is free indeed.

Let's discuss Jerusalem and Jesus. In the text, Jesus was sitting on the Mount of Olives with His disciples and said, "Oh, Jerusalem, how often I wanted to gather your children together, the way a hen gathers her chicks under her wings and you were unwilling' Now your house is being left to your desolate . . . You shall not see Me until you say. 'Blessed is He who comes in the name of the Lord!'"

Jesus wept for Jerusalem. He saw into the future what was going to happen to the Jewish people in Jerusalem. He saw that thirty-eight years later Titus and the Roman legions, exceeding 50,000 troops, surrounded the city of Jerusalem and laid siege to the city, producing massive starvation.

Luke 21:20 says, "When you see Jerusalem surrounded by armies—flee and know that the desolation is about to happen." The historian Josephus tells the story of Roman soldiers going from house to house killing the survivors of the siege. They were killing off the remainder of people too weakened by starvation to defend themselves. A soldier walked into the home of a mother who was eating her infant child, and even he backed out of that home, being repulsed by the scene. Josephus recites that 1.1 million people died there when Jerusalem was demolished and the temple torn down. Jesus saw that and He wept! Remember His going up to Calvary, He saw the women weeping and He said, "Daughters of Jerusalem, do not weep for Me, but for yourselves, and for your children" (Luke 23:8). Why? Because He knew and said, "Blessed are the barren wombs that never bore, and breast which never nursed" (Luke 23:21). The message - blessed is the woman who has no child, because when the Romans arrive you will fight over that child as to who will eat the child.

Jesus wept when He saw the crusades in 1099 where nine hundred plus (900+) Jews were burned alive in their synagogue. The crusaders marched under the sign of the cross and herded Jewish men, women and children into their synagogue, set it on fire, and cremated them while the crusaders sang, "Christ, We Adore Thee." There were seven major Roman Crusades in which the Jews were butchered from Europe to Jerusalem and back from Jerusalem to Europe. Jesus saw that and wept.

He wept when he saw the Spanish Inquisition operate. There the Roman Church authorities dug up the bones of dead Jews and put them on trial. Since the dead Jews were not present or able to represent themselves, the Roman Church expropriated all their wealth and placed it in their treasury.

Jesus saw the Hitler Holocaust and the systematic murder of six million Jews. Jesus wept when He saw the Jews being forced in this century out of their homes in Gaza to fulfill the anti-biblical political pipe dream of the so-called "Roadmap to Peace."

Jesus wept when He saw the coming of the Antichrist in the near future. Antichrist is a false messiah who will come out of Europe and make a seven year peace treaty with Israel. Then three the antichrist will break that treaty and and one half years later, will set up his image in the city of Jerusalem for the whole world to worship. Anyone who will not worship him will be executed. Jesus saw that and wept. The Antichrist is coming soon. But know this — the tears of Jesus over the situation confronting the Jews and the abuse of Israel are about to stop because the Lamb of God discussed in Matthew is about to return as the Lion of the Tribe of Judah. The Babe in Bethlehem's manger is about to return as King of Kings and Lord of Lords. The Rabbi who rode the donkey in the streets of Jerusalem and who was crucified a week later is about to ride through the clouds of heaven on a white horse, followed by the armies of heaven which are assembled there, and on His head shall be a crown — The King of Kings and Lord of Lords. He is going to rule this earth for one thousand years from the Temple Mount of His Father King David in the city of Jerusalem. He is going to rule the earth with a rod of iron. That means He is not going to ask the U. S. Supreme Court if it is allowable to pray: He is not going to ask the ACLU (American Civil Liberties Union) if the Ten Commandments can be posted or recited. We will be ruled by the law of the Living God without Apology. Give him Praise! The Nazarene that was dragged before Herod and Pilate will have kings, queens, emperors, presidents, prime ministers, senators, congressmen, the rich and the mighty, and the powerful line LIP and bow before Him. Every knee shall bow and every tongue shall confess that He, Jesus, is Lord to the glory of God the Father. It is going to happen in the city of Jerusalem.

Let us review the seven signs of His coming.

1. The rebirth of Israel. Jesus told His disciples in Matthew 24:32, "Now learn' the parable of the fig tree (Israel). When you see the branch begin again to bloom (meaning that it is dead for a while), you will know that my coming is even at the door." In the Bible that means that His hand is on the doorknob.

    When the Romans crushed Jerusalem in 70 AD, the Diaspora (the scattering of the Jews) began. Figuratively the fig tree died. On May 15, 1948, the fig tree was reborn in a day, as was prophesied by Isaiah 66:8. The tree is blooming again. Israel is alive! The King of Glory is on His way! If you listen closely, you can hear the footsteps of Messiah shuffling through the clouds of heaven. Messiah is coming.

2. The second sign of his coming is the birth of nuclear warfare. Before the birth of nuclear warfare, there was a portion of prophetic scripture that was a mystery to my father's generation. We wondered how those mysteries could be a possibility. Today, however, things are tragically clear as the world races toward Armageddon. Zechariah 14:12 says, "And this is the plague that the Lord shall send on all who come to fight against Jerusalem. Their flesh shall consume away while they stand on their feet, and their eyes shall consume away in their sockets, and their tongues shall consume away in their mouths." No one really comprehended that scripture verse. When the atomic bomb was created, then we began to understand it. Next came the hydrogen bomb that can produce the heat of 150,000,000 degrees Fahrenheit in one millionth of a second. With the explosion of a hydrogen bomb, it is now easy to envision how the tongue can be consumed in its mouth and eyes melt in the sockets before your corpse can hit the ground. We know Iran at the present is working on a nuclear weapon, and they are predicted to soon have such a weapon. It appears that war is in the near future. Israel has no choice but to defend itself against Iran whose leaders have announced that Israel should be eliminated. Israel does not owe it to the world to commit political suicide for the sake of fulfilling the "Roadmap to Peace." Iran will use those weapons on Israel, and anyone who is smart enough to wave and say bye, bye, knows that. Diplomacy is failing, and Iran ' from Washington, will continue to fail. Iran gives every indication that diplomacy Berlin, Paris, and Rome. Russia is helping Iran to develop the bomb because that is where many of their unemployed nuclear scientists have gone to work. Life as we know it today will be different in the near future, It is going to be rough. Get ready and get right with Jesus. It is going to happen.

3. The third sign is the knowledge explosion. Daniel 12:4 says, "But you Daniel, shut up the words and seal the book even to the time of the end when many shall run to and fro (like the large city traffic jams) and knowledge shall be greatly increased." Knowledge shall be greatly increased is properly translated as "knowledge explosion." Our generation is the only one that has had a knowledge explosion. From the

time of the Garden of Eden to the twentieth century, transportation was basically by horseback. Then came the wagons, cars, aircraft and finally jet aircraft, in that order. Today you can cross the world in the time it previously required to cross over a city. Consider communications. From the time of the Garden of Eden to the twentieth century, it was fundamentally the same. Then came the telegraph, radio, telephone, television and today sky pagers, in that order. Today you can reach and communicate with a passenger in an airplane flying on the other side of the world. Just imagine — telephone, telegraph, tell a person — it goes everywhere.

Consider medical science: from the Garden of Eden to the twentieth century, there was relatively little change. There is some evidence that in Roman times medical science was more advanced than some of what we have today. Now we are experiencing a medical explosion. We can keep alive and breathing with machines and miracle drugs long after the body cannot function normally. Your child can get on a computer and tap into all the data information available. Of course, most of it is not good for them, but it is available. Knowledge without God produces only an intellectual barbarian. Knowledge has not produced a perfect world. d We are that generation of whom the Bible speaks as "ever learning but never coming to the knowledge of truth." What is truth? It is not something. The truth Someone. Jesus said, "I am the Way the 4:6 Truth and the Life" (John 14:6). We Americans must know the truth.

4. The Fourth sign is Exodus 2. Jeremiah 23:7 reads: "Therefore the days are coming when they will no more say 'As the Lord lives which brought us up out of Egypt (Exodus 1), but they shall say as the Lord lives that brought us up form the north country (We all know that north of Jerusalem is Russia.) that they may dwell in our land (Israel)."

The re-gathering of Russian Jews to Jerusalem is a fulfillment of Jeremiah 23. It is an obvious sign that we are approaching the end of the age. I personally have contributed to efforts to help pay for those flights taking Russian Jews to Israel, but there are organizations contributing mightily to bring about this prophetic fulfillment. This will continue until the Russians close the doors or the Trumpet of God sounds. It is the will of God for our generation.

5. The fifth sign is that Jerusalem is no longer under Gentile rule. Luke 21:24 states, "And Jerusalem shall be trodden down by Gentiles until the time of the Gentiles be fulfilled." We all know that the Jewish people gained control of Jerusalem in the six day war of 1967. Jesus said that generation would not pass until all had been fulfilled. Another obvious sign that we are approaching the end of the age. Psalm 102:16 recites, "When the Lord shall build up Jerusalem He shall appear in all of His glory." Jerusalem is the city of God. He has chosen Jerusalem (Zion). He has declared it as His habitation.

6. The sixth sign is the invention of international television. Again here is another verse that was a mystery to my father's generation. Revelation 11:9, 10 describes the two witnesses who will be killed by the Antichrist and will lie dead in the streets of Jerusalem for three days. The world will be witnesses are alive the people will exchange gifts. But then the Bible says that the world will see them at one time. How can that be? Surely not via newspapers. One time means everyone can see them at the same instance. Not possible in 1940-1950-1960. Then came the satellite television and it became instantly possible that all could view an event in the world at the same time. We will be able to see Elijah and Enoch lying in the streets of Jerusalem. Those of us in heaven will be looking down on the event; the rest of you will be on earth watching CNN, NBC or ABC.

7. The seven sign is the sign of deception. Jesus said in Matthew 24:4, "Take heed that no man deceive you." Secular humanism is deception since it teaches there is no right or wrong. It is the devil's theology. Secular humanism has produced a generation of AIDS and abortion and filled our penitentiaries and divorce courts. Why? Because no one is responsible for their own predicament. It's my mother's fault, daddy's fault or the government's fault is their response. But you alone are responsible for your situation. You are where you are because you are what you are!

New Age is deception. Harmonizing with a glass of crystal will produce laryngitis, but it will not get you to the Lord of glory. That's deception. Neo-environmentalism and worshipping "Mother Earth" as God is paganism, pantheism and deception. Because of the neo-environmental fanatics, you are paying more than $3.00 for a gallon of gasoline. They prefer protecting some bug or fish to setting America free from the bondage of foreign oil. That prevents oil drilling in "environmentally sensitive areas" so as to avoid the possibility of annoying a bug, bird or animal. Here is an example: a pastor friend told me about his church's property located in the center of a large American city. At the edge of the church property is an acre of land set aside unused and surrounded by a chain fence. They need to expand the church and need the property to grow. But the acre is environmentally protected by our government. Why? Because forty feet below the surface in a little cave lives a bug called a "blind beetle." It is about one inch long and is on the "endangered species" list. Our government says you shall not disturb that blind beetle. The beetle therefore keeps that church from using that property for which they have paid handsomely.

The Apostate Church is deception. America is being spiritually sedated with what I call a "feel good" gospel. The objective to preaching is to make people feel good without being good; to explain their sin rather than to confront their sin; to generate a "hot tub" Christianity that takes no stand against the difficult moral issues of our time. This is a church that has lost its willingness to be the salt and light. Pulpits in America are being constantly filled with reverend "cotton candy," and pastors are preaching a "feel good" theology, sending their congregations dancing out the front doors and headed for the fires of hell. That is because they have never defined sin, have refused to confront sin, and therefore they are becoming a part of the Apostate Church. Jesus responded to the Apostate Church when they asked, "Lord, have we not done wonderful things in your name?" by saying, Depart from Me workers of iniquity — I never knew you." That is going to happen on the day of judgment.

We are the terminal generation. Jesus is coming much sooner than you think, that is why I tell you today that if Jesus doesn't come this week, I will see you next Sunday. I, as many feel down deep in my soul He is near, and I see His hand on horn to your lips the doorknob pulling it open while saying to Gabriel — "Put the horn to your lips and give us a mighty blast." The dead in Christ are going to rise and we shall meet the Lord in the air, and we who are alive and remaining shall fly into the presence of God. Hallelujah!

Stand please.

How many of you can say — "Preacher, if the Lord Jesus were to come within the next sixty seconds for me, I am not ready?" If that describes you, please hold up your hand. I will pray for you where you are — God can save you right there. I see many, many hands.

Pray this prayer with me —

Lord, in the name of Jesus Christ, I ask you to forgive me of all my sins, and wash my soul in the Blood of Calvary's Lamb, Our Lord Jesus Christ. I surrender my life, my heart, my mind and my body to your service from this day forward. Father, from this day forward, You are the Lord of all that I possess. Direct every step that I take, in all my tomorrows and now, in the name of Jesus. I am saved and my sins are forgiven; they are blotted out never to be remembered against me. I am on my way to heaven because Christ is Savior and Lord; Amen.

Bless His Name —The King is Coming!

Hold up your hands for a blessing.

Now may the Lord bless you and May the Lord keep you, and may the Lord make His face to shine upon you, and may the Lord be gracious unto you. May you prepare your, heart, your soul, and your family for the greatest event the world will ever see — the coming of the Son of God in the clouds of heaven. He is coming sooner than you can think or imagine. Be not dismayed by the cares of this earth for they will be instantly forgotten at the sounding of the trumpet and the gathering of the Bride in the presence of God. In Jesus' name, we pray and say hallelujah!

This powerful sermon was written by brother Dr. Paul Shimek, Jr. a servant of God.

Question: How are these sermons promoting, pronouncing, propelling, prospering, and providential to the readers Let me tell you.

- Promoting —To help further promote the growth of those If you who are in the Word or want the Word within them. abide in me, and my words abide in you, you shall ask what you will, and it will be done unto you" (John 15:7).

- Pronouncing — God always remember what He says. He responds favorably to you when you remember what He says. These sermons declare official that God's word is unmistakable true. "For the word of the Lord is right; and all his works are done in truth" (Psalm 33:4).

- Propelling — They will help to supply the needed fuel for chose who really wane co love and obey the King. "And you shall seek me, and find me, when you shall search for me with all your heart" (Jeremiah 29:13).

- Prospering — Hopefully one will commie his or her work; his or her all to God. "By humility and fear of the Lord are riches, honor, and life" (Proverbs 22:4).

- Providential - God is Provident. One must seek the prudent (wise, careful) guidance of God. He sees all and knows all. "And it shall come to pass, that before they call, I will answer; and while they are yet speaking, I will hear" (Isaiah 65:24).

I HAVE CALLED THEE BY NAME: THOU ART MINE

ISAIAH 43: 1b

ABOUT THE AUTHOR

The Hindu Philosopher Ramakrisna voiced a fable about a tiger cub that was separated from his mother and fellow tigers. Goats had adopted him and raised him as if he were a goat. So, instead of his roaring like a lion, he bleated softly. He had been cut off from his true identity. I have asked myself, "How many times have I been cut off from my true identity?" "How many times have I forgotten who I am in Christ?" Fortunately, now I know who I am and how His power works within me.

I remember my visiting Nassau. While we were eating in a restaurant within the motel, my friend girl and I were approached by a worker in the motel. She asked us several questions about ourselves. The she wrote on a piece of paper the name of the lady we should contact in order to tour the millionaires' suites. Why? We didn't know. We did follow the directions. On the day of our tour, needless to say, I asked that others join us because if we were to be blessed, I wanted others blessed as well. My wish was granted. The tour guide said that she could not understand why we were privileged to visit this floor because "No one, not even salesmen are allowed to visit this area. Only those who had five hundred thousand dollars or more in the hotel bank are allowed on this floor." I cried to explain to her as we enjoyed the tour that my Father was very, very, rich. He owns the cattle on a thousand of hills. He is rich. Therefore, it isn't unusual for my having been invited to visit a wealthy area. She didn't understand. But I knew my Father, and I knew my identity.

In preparing this book for your reading, I invoked the opportunity to reflect upon some of my spiritual experiences that helped prepare me for the beliefs I hold true. I was born in Houston, Texas, and grew up in Pensacola, Florida. My mother and father moved to Chicago where a speeding car killed my father as he stood on the corner waiting to cross the street. After my father's death, my mother moved to Florida to join her parents. She completed two years of college at Alabama State and taught in a one-room school for several years. During this period, I was left with my grandparents. My grandmother was from the West Indies; my grandfather was half Native American and half French living in French Town in New Orleans. He was a devout Catholic who met my grandmother (a Methodist) in New Orleans and the two were married. I was told that they moved to Florida where he worked for the Louisville and Nashville Railroad Company. I remember as a very young girl our home was spotless. In the backyard, we had a large chicken coop with roosters and hens, plenty of fruit trees and grape vines. There were large piles of wood stock stacked high within our yard. After my grandfather retired from the railroad, he sold wood to all who needed it. In the front yard, there were oleander trees and other flowers. Our house was wood with a concrete porch. My grandparents owned the house next door, as well. Prior to my entering school, my grandmother died and my mother had to move in with us. She had remarried and had a baby girl. There were several other children born to that union...all of us were close. As the children them moved to Illinois and got good jobs. I remained in Florida. My sister was thirty-six years old when she died and three of my brothers passed, also. In Florida, there were several ethnic groups living on the same block in the neighborhood in which we lived (i.e., Native Americans, African Americans, called Negroes at that time, Caucasians, and even one Greek family). As children we all played together, my friend Jeannie even spent many nights with me, but the African American children attended the old wooden white school with marked up books and used desks. The one joy in attending that elementary school is that the teachers taught well and learning wasn't an option. It was a demand. I remembered only one boy that was slow in reading. Everyone in the whole school read and wrote, pledged allegiance to the flag and prayed.

At home my grandfather invited me to read the Bible to him each day. I read and he interpreted what I had read. This was my first real introduction to God. We got on our knees and prayed every night but God seemed so far away except when the large cumulus clouds would form. If I were asked to go to the store, I would watch the clouds all the way because I heard the older folks that visited our home talk about God, and that Jesus would come back in a cloud to collect all of His own. In my walking to the store, I would watch the clouds to see if He were coining through them. I even imagined the cloud swooping down to pick me up. For a long time I told no one about this image. Then one day, I confessed to my "daddy" (grandfather) my thoughts. He embraced me and told me what the Bible said about Jesus' return. I felt better about the clouds, but I must admit that I was suspicious of them. My grandfather focused upon my spiritual endeavors. He was a real Christian and didn't want anyone mistreated, gossiping, lying, nor breaking the Commandments. He was so handsome but he didn't focus on the outward appearance of a person, he focused on the behavior of the individual. He taught me to read the Bible daily, especially the Psalms. He made sure I understood the necessity of reading the Bible and Praying. Until this day, I always spend quality time reading and praying. In fact, each day I arise between 4:15 and 4:30 to begin my reading. At 5:00 a.m. my prayer partner and I spend a minimum of one hour in prayer on the telephone.

I begin working in the Methodist Church at an early age. One night my friends and I attended a Baptist revival. All of the young folks had to sit on the front row. The preacher told us that we were going to hell. We were afraid and all of us instantaneously jump up and joined the church. We went home, told our parents and they prepared us for baptism. Shortly afterward, we were baptized in the Gulf of Mexico, but we never went back to that church. Each of us went to our home church. I went to the church in which I grew up, and I worked in many capacities---as a teacher, lay leader, local pastor, and lead pastor of the church, as well. I have served on the local and conference levels of the church until my matriculation at a school of theology, many years later. Now, I am back working again at home. However, I know that God has a mighty job for me to do and I will do it in Jesus' name. I have a passion for Jesus, and God has given me gifts and grace to glorify Him. Many of you reading this now have been given work or will be given work to do for God. Let no man or woman stop you! It is my belief that God is preparing a mighty army for His work to be done.

Who am I? As I look back on my young adult life, I recall my working in the laundry and on weekends at a nightclub. As a teenager, I married a serviceman. I met him at the club where I worked and really didn't want to talk with him because servicemen had a bad reputation in my hometown. He convinced me that he was different and for several years he was. He didn't want me to work or attend college, but after two children the spirit within me informed me to acquire a college education. I attended the junior college at home. After graduation, I received a scholarship to attend a four-year college. Graduating from this college, my children and that have been formative. These boards and communities helped the marginalized and the disinherited on the local and state levels. I even served on a committee on the national level. For eighteen years, I had a jail ministry. I have received many awards, honors, recognition. I received my Ph.D from Florida State University, and Master in Theology from Emory University all which are good but more importantly is my love for God, my family, friends and others. I just want to be a servant and friend. Presently, I have a radio ministry in Pensacola, Florida, and work with many volunteer agencies. I am constantly invited to speak on many occasions.

Bell Hooks in Teaching to Transgress states that during the time between ending one project and beginning another, she always has a crisis of meaning. Hooks says, "I begin to wonder what my life is all about and what I have been put on this earth to do. It is as though immersed in a project I lose all sense of myself and must then, when the work is done, rediscover who I am and where I am going." Frequently, I have to say, "Okay, God I need your help to remember who I am, whose I am and what am I to do now." I had to recall that I am a minister! People questioned my returning to seminary at my age. I knew that I was in the right place, at the right time, for the right reason, meeting the right people all in the will of God. When I completed my studies, I was asked to go to take parish. I felt that God was leading me into the field of Evangelism. Therefore,

I had to seek God's guidance and the guidance of others that knew the territory, well. After receiving the needed advice from two former district superintendents, a pastor having served the charge, and God, I discovered that this assignment had dangerous elements. I was highly disappointed and badly hurt chat I was not given another assignment. And that I was approaching the age of retirement. I just did not fit the mold.

Nevertheless, God has he given mold. me a great work to do; age, ethnicity and nothing else will make a difference. The Bible tells us of great men and women who did miraculous deeds when they became of a good age. Read the Bible and discover these men and women of God. Who am P I am a child of God with a passion to do the will of God!

Why have I written this segment? I feel that if you know a bit about the author, you will better appreciate his or her book(s). READ and ENJOY WHAT GOD IS SAYING TO YOU THROUGH THIS BOOK.

Addie June Hall

NOTES

Foreword

1. Brougknight, B. Sermon illustrations —www. Sermon.com (June 24, 2001)
2. Hoard, W.B. Outstanding Black Sermons, Volume 2, (Valley Forge: Judson Press, 1979), pp.12-13.
3. Mitchell, H. Black Preaching (New York: J.B. Lippincott, 1970), p. 203.
4. Moyd, H. The Sacred Art: Preaching and Theology (Valley Forge: Judson Press, 1995), p.5.
5. Roberts, J.R. Black Theology in Dialogue (Philadelphia: West Press, 1987), p. 84.

Love Your Wife and Save Your Life

1. Adams, J.E. From Forgiven to Forgiving (New York: Calvary Press) Reprinted in Free Grace Broadcaster, A Ministry of Mt. Zion Bible Church, Pensacola, FL 2003, p. 3
2. Froehle, V.A. Loving Yourself More . . . 101 Meditations for Women (Notre Dame, IN: Ave Maria Press, 1997), p. 110.
3. 3. Hall, A.J. The Wife / The Other Woman (Shippensburg, PA: Companion Press, 1995)
4. Hart, A. D. Growing Up Divorced (Ann Arbor, MI: Servant Publication, 1991), p. 43.
5. Williams, D. Sisters in the Wilderness (Maryknoll, NY: Orbis Books, 1993), (Gathered Inspirations from reading Hager's story) pp.15-31.

Walking in Love
1. Bondi, R. To Love As God Loves (Philadelphia, PA: Fortress Press, 1987), pp. 23, 107-108.
2. Buechner, F. The Magnificent Defeat (San Francisco, CA: Harper Collins, May, 1985) p. 105.
3. Skinner, Sr. J. Seeing With the Heart (Chicago, IL: Urban Ministries, 1996), (Inspirational Reading)
4. Thurman, H. Jesus and the Disinherited (Nashville, TN: Abingdon Press, 1949), p.89.

Why Pray? Prayer Changes Your Life and Circumstances
1. Jones, E. Stanley. Liberating Ministry from the Success Syndrome (K. Hughes: Carol Stream, IL: Tyndale Publishing Company, 1988), p.73.
2. Johnson, J. K. Why Christians Sin? (Grand, MI: Discovery House: 1992), p.129.
3. The illustrations were taken from Brett Blair Sermon Illustrations, July 2001. Story from Paul Harvey Comment and News (date unknown).
4. The Kneeling Christians, Clarion Classics (Grand, MI: Zondervan Publishing House) pp.79-80.
5. Today in the Word (January, 1990) p. 36.

God Forgives Sins, Ask Him
1. Illustration of Paco was taken from Bits and Pieces. (October 15, 1992) p. 13.
2. Scott, C. F. Rev, Sermon on the Woman Caught in Adultery (First Presbyterian Church Of Maitland, Fl March 18, 2001), used excerpts.
3. Readings from Evelyn Lein. As We Forgive Those (Unity, 1987)
4. Teaching from Dr. J. B, Nichols, serving as pastor of St. Paul UMC, (Pensacola, Fl. 1977,1978), (I served under his leadership).
5. www. Bible Verses and Trivia _ Got A Heavy, Slimy Sack of Potatoes? (October 11, 2002)
6. www. Children Globe Corn: Home

Phenomenal Women Using Their Talents for God
1. Angelou, Maya, et.al. The Complete Collected Poems of Maya Angelou. (Random House, Inc. August, 1994, First Edition / printing 1978)
2. Ebony Magazine. 100 Most Fascinating Black Women of the 20th Century. (March, 1999).
3. Ebony magazine. 100 Most Important Blacks in the World in the 20th Century (March, 1999).
4. Women International Net Magazine, Issue 44, (June 2001).
5. Women's History. http://womenhistory.about.corn

What If God Had An Answering Machine?
1. Sheffield, R.L. Stimineifruit (The CSS Publishing Company 1994, 0-7880-0042-x).

Jesus Blesses The Little Children
1. Children and Poverty: An Episcopal Initiative (1996), www.njumc.org/bicp.html
2. The Bishop's Initiative: Children and Poverty 1996 www.cpcumc.org/unwitness/children.html
3. Wesley, John. Sermons. http://gbgm-umc.org/umhistory/ wesley/ sermons/

God Chose Powerless People for Powerful Tasks
1. Duncan, K. "The Amazing Law of Influence." (Greatna, LA: Pelican Publishing Company, 2001).
2. Nigro, J.A. " The Ordinary Person That God Uses " (Straight Path Ministries, Paramus, NJ).
3. Osborne, C. " A Letter to Jesus " (Printed in Yorkfellows Newsletter, 1991), Reprinted in the United Methodist Christian Advocate, 1992.

Lord Spare My Family and All That We Possess
1. The New King Version of the Holy Bible (Atlanta, GA: Thomas Nelson Publishers, 1985).

2. The Revised Standard Version of the King James Bible (Atlanta, GA: Thomas Nelson Publishers, 1990).

The Final Judgment of Nations / Gentile Nations
1. Townsend, J. Sermon of The Sheep and Goats (2003), p. 17 (This sermon was sent to me by Dr. Townsend and I was given permission to use quotes when needed).

The Lord Is on My Side; I Will Not Fear
1. Introduction Illustrations --- The Tower Chimes of the First United Methodist Church (Vol. 7, Dr. Karl K. Stegall, Pastor, Montgomery, Alabama).
2. Jones, E. S. Transformed by Thorns (Republished by Grant Martin, Colorado, Springs, CL: Chariot Victor Books: June, 1985), p. 95
3. Rivers, M. The statement was reported within the Dallas Morning News. (Dallas, TX: May 20, 1984).
4. The New King James Version of The Holy Bible (Nashville, TN: 1985).
5. The New Revised Standard Version of The Holy Bible (Nashville, TN: 1990).

Repent America and Pray
1. Levitt, Zola. Zola Levitt Ministries (Dallas, TX: October, 2001).
2. The Holy Bible Christian Life Edition, The New King Version (Atlanta, GA: Thomas Nelson Publishers, 1985).

Jerusalem: Countdown to Crises

With Dr. Paul Shimek permission, I have selected excerpts from his sermon to include within this book. Dr. Shimek's autobiograply is included. His sermon was written in January, 2007.